Vampire – The Quest for Truth

Charmain Marie Mitchell

Publisher: Cmmpublishing, Petersfield, Hampshire, UK.

First published in the UK, US, and worldwide, in August 2014

Edition One

ISBN-13: 978-1502395733

ISBN-10: 1502395738

<<<<>>>>

Index

Other books by Author   5

Dedication   6

Part I

Chapter one   7

Part II

Chapter two   12

Chapter three   24

Chapter four   28

Chapter five   38

Chaper six   42

Chapter seven   47

Chapter eight   54

Chapter nine   59

Chapter ten   61

Chapter eleven   66

Part III

Chapter twelve   69

Chapter thirteen   74

Chapter fourteen   79

Part IV

Chapter fifteen   85

Chapter sixteen   89

Chapter seventeen   94

Chapter eighteen   98

Chapter nineteen   100

Chapter twenty   105

Chapter twenty one   110

Part V

Chapter twenty two   117

Chapter twenty three   124

Chapter twenty four   129

Chapter twenty five   136

Chapter twenty six   141

Coming soon   144

Excerpt from Death Whispers   145

About the author   169

Other books by Charmain Marie Mitchell

Lust For Blood

Vampire – In the Beginning

Death Whispers – Book One of the Mary
Howard Series

Vampire – Child Of Destiny

Vampire – Gwens Journels 1542 – 1627 –
Vampire Series books 1, 2 and 3
combined.

For my beautiful daughter-in-law Joanne –
now you can read it x

As usual I'd like to say a huge thank you to
my four beautiful children, my mum and
dad, and to my partner Mike – Love you
all lots and lots. And a huge thank you to
Julia Gibbs (Juliaproofreader) – you were
great – as always.

Part One

Chapter One

Gwen

Present Day

Today I browsed through the second journal of my memoirs, and I realised something that I should have realised a long time ago—I am a hypocrite! I look at my own words floating in front of my eyes and I read about how I've murdered, plundered, and pillaged, and then I cringe at how I justify my actions. I am no better than Robert or Louis; in fact, I can now see that I am actually probably worse. You see, at least they admit and accept what they are, which is something that I've never been able to do.

I pretend that I am so good, and that I would rather die than live in the sadistic world that is the life of a vampire. However, this is obviously so untrue, because if it were true, well then, surely I would have done the world a favour and killed myself a long time ago?

Of course, I see now that I will never take my own life.

I lie to myself and find excuses for why I must continue, why I must live, but I've failed to see, up until now that is, that I choose to live simply because I want to.

I have therefore made a vow. I will never again feel sorry for my actions, and I will accept the person that I am. After all, I have no other choice, because I now know with all certainty that I will live forever, and for once instead of feeling remorse, I will feel liberated—I can finally be the woman that I was always meant to be.

I also realise that I have tried to be a better person, and just because I have failed on countless occasions, it doesn't mean that I am any worse for my failures; it just shows me that I was in fact once human, and failing is a trait that seems somewhat hard to shake. Yes I have killed, but then that is the nature of the beast. I am a vampire and I have lived this way for the majority of my life, and although I do try and fight against it, I am now, and always will be very much a killer.

In some ways I regret that I have spent so many years wallowing in self-pity. Those years, I now know, could have been spent in more worthwhile pursuits, but instead, being the person that I am, I have wasted them.

I shudder to think how many discoveries I could have made if I had not lived my life shrouded by guilt. I look back with true regret, at the lost years that I wasted. Years that could have been used in pursuit of my quest. Ah, but I am getting ahead of myself. The quest comes later - much later.

Instead my story continues with that of my beautiful granddaughter, Rose. Of the life we made together and the happiness we shared. I cannot tell you how much I would love to go back to the first day I held her in my arms, albeit with Robert breathing down my neck. It was a magical day, for it was the day I regained my family. Of course, I had known by then that I had lost my son to Robert. Henry, I knew, was intent on fulfilling the prophecy that Robert had foretold to me when he gave me the choice of living or dying on that fateful day so many years ago. However, when I looked into Rose's eyes, and saw my own staring back at me, I knew that I was part of her future, and she was mine. I killed Matilda in order to establish our future together and in doing so made Robert, and my son Henry, my enemies for all time.

Not a day goes by when I do not miss Rose and her beauty and grace.

She was like an angel to my devil, and the soothing water that heals the burn. Everything in my life became Rose, and the day we stepped off that weather-worn ship onto the French shore, and I held her fragile beauty in my arms, was the first day of my new life. The life we shared, a time that was so tantalisingly short, but so overwhelmingly perfect.

Rose was taught to write in a journal. Her journal was considered part of her education, and was an everyday occurrence required by her tutor, Pierre. At the time I thought it was a ridiculous waste of time, but I changed my mind the day I found this beautiful part of her. I still read it, and sometimes I can imagine her; sitting in front of me, busily writing down all of her precious thoughts and secrets. Thoughts and secrets, which I now know word by word, and treasure beyond anything that I own.

In the following pages Rose will tell her story in her own words, because although this is my story, my beautiful girl's life was so entangled in my own. Of course, with the knowledge of years I look back and realise that I could have changed her future if I had paid more attention.

Alas, hindsight is a wondrous thing, and is a burden that serves as a lesson for us to learn from. Do we always learn from it? I'm not so sure, and I believe that given the same set of circumstances I would have probably done the same things again.

Ah, but I so wish that I had acted differently. However, wishes are dreams, and dreams are a luxury that I know from experience rarely come to fruition. Nevertheless, one thing I know with certainty: 'To look to the future, we must always look to the past.' If only I had known that back then! Alas, I cannot change any of the past, but I can share it with you in the hope that you benefit from my folly and in doing so, hopefully, you will not make the same mistakes that I made. So, for now at least, I put down my pen, and leave you to read the story of Rose......

Part 2

Chapter Two

Rose

Summer of 1574

I have been ordered to write about my life in this journal by my tutor, Pierre. How strange it is, that thoughts flow through my mind all of the time, but when asked to write them down, I cannot think of one thing to write about. After sitting for a long time in front of my blank page, I told Pierre of my dilemma. He barked out a laugh, and replied, "But, mademoiselle, there you have your beginning, write that you know not what to write about...you will see that once you start, you will find it difficult to stop!"

I shook my head in bewilderment. Sometimes Pierre talked in riddles.
"I cannot see why I must write in a stupid journal anyway..." I stated petulantly.
"Aww...But one day you will, mademoiselle...One day when you are old, you will wish to read about your youth...the excitement of being young. Oui.... then you will thank Pierre..."

"Bah...that is silly..." I whined, "I do nothing exciting for me to write about...I believe I shall be very bored if I read it when I am old!" I snapped.

"Ah..." Pierre laughed again. "Nevertheless, you shall write, mademoiselle...no more arguments, oui..."

It was obvious from the way he placed his hands on his hips and tapped his foot with ill-concealed irritation that I was not going to win the battle. So I tried to smile nicely, and once more looked at the blank pages of the journal. Of course, although it pains me to say it, Pierre was correct, and once I started to write—I found it difficult to stop.

My name is Rose Le Cadeau and I live in a large chateau, in a remote stretch of countryside several miles from the town of Bordeaux. I choose to introduce myself because after thinking about the reasons for writing in this journal, I was struck by the fact that in years to come my thoughts might be read by a stranger, and I have concluded that they would wish to know who they are reading about. After all, I would wish to know, and would find it very frustrating to read about someone without a name.

I will be fourteen on All Hallows Eve.

Maman tells me this is a day that people fear evil spirits in England—the place of my birth. However, in France, it is a day to remember the spirits of departed loved ones, and it is this meaning that I prefer. I am surrounded by people that I love and who love me in return, but I love none like Maman. She says that our surname means 'the gift', and to her that is what I am. She always laughs gaily when I state that she is also my gift from God, but sometimes it seems that her laughter is false and I sense that sadness is hidden somewhere in the depths of her giggles.

Her sadness, I believe, is due to the death of my father. We moved to France when I was just a very small baby. I have heard the story so many times, but still I love to hear it.

The tragic tale of how my father's enemy, the cruel and demonic Lord Robert Vanike, arrived at our former home one freezing cold night in November. The men bitterly quarrelled over the ownership of land that bordered both of their estates. The quarrel turned very violent, and the evil and despised Lord Vanike, who was by this time in a blistering rage, murdered my father by stabbing him through the heart.

I cannot recall how many times I have imagined the terrible bloody scene of my father dying, or how many times I have cried at the thought of him being murdered by such a cruel and heartless man, but the feeling of loss never fades. Nor does the overwhelming feeling of love and gratitude for my beautiful Maman; because although she was alone and at the mercy of the evil lord, she found the courage to escape and lead us both to safety. Maman travelled all through the night on horseback with me, just a small babe in arms, tied to her slight frame. She rode, for many tortuous miles, non-stop until we wearily reached Dover. From Dover we boarded a waiting ship, and thus we travelled to France, and onward to Bordeaux where we took up residence in my father's chateau.

I cannot deny that I love the Chateau Cadeau—it is the only home I have ever known. However, I sometimes wish that we could visit England, how I would love to explore our old home, but Maman says that it is unsafe for us to do so. She says that the evil Lord Vanike will capture us and hold us under guard, and so we have no choice but to remain in France.

However, I cannot pretend that I do not daydream of the day I shall return to the country of my birth, or the day I shall avenge my father's death. I, of course, must keep my dream to myself. Maman would be very angry if I even mentioned to her that I have future hopes of returning to England. And I believe that she would even resort to keeping me under lock and key if she was to discover my intentions of one day returning.

I love Maman so very much, but I cannot deny the fact that she can be very fierce, or that no one in the chateau ever disobeys her commands. I sometimes see the servants sneak past her, and then I witness them hurriedly make the sign of the cross—an action they do when they hope to protect themselves against evil. I find their fear amusing, and sometimes find that I must pinch myself in order to stop giggling. I know they fear her, and I also know that she would never harm them, but even I am not sure how she would react to knowing the fact that the servants think she is a devil—and so I ignore their fear.

I sometimes wonder if it is Maman's beauty which frightens the servants so, because she is, quite literally, the most beautiful woman I, and I am sure most of them, have ever seen.

She remains so young looking, and we have on many occasions been mistaken for sisters. I am always amused when I hear people exclaim in startled surprise that they are unable to believe that she is my maman. Maman, however, does not find their startled protests amusing; in fact, it seems to irritate her greatly, so much so that sometimes I have seen her grow quite angry at the fact. Many times I have said, "Maman, please...it is a compliment, is it not?" But my cajoling doesn't ease her anger, if anything it can make it worse, and of late, because of her obvious discomfort, I have refrained from commenting when circumstances such as these arise.

Nonetheless, growing up in the protected confines of the Chateau Cadeau was truly magical, and for me, as a small child, it resembled a majestic kingdom. I remember, so clearly, pretending to be a beautiful princess reigning over my loyal subjects. I imagined myself to be just like Queen Elizabeth, the young and beautiful queen of England, and that my people fiercely loved and protected me. Now and then I would manage to persuade Maman to join in, and she would play the role of Elizabeth's sister—the evil Bloody Mary.

Maman would sometimes protest that she was bored with always playing the role of the evil sister, to which I would argue that I was fair in colouring just like Elizabeth, and she was dark like Queen Mary. And so it was more authentic if we continued to maintain our usual roles. Maman would laugh heartily at my remark, often stating that I was very cunning and that it would serve me well if the need should arise. I never really understood her remark, but I would smile and laugh just the same, for I loved to make her proud and to see her happy.

It was about this time that I started to realise that I differed greatly from Maman in looks, we shared the same eyes, but other than that we were quite different in appearance.

"Maman..." I once asked her, "Do I look like mon père?"

"Why do you say that, my love...?" she replied lightly, but I noticed how she had sat up straighter in her chair, and how her eyes became more watchful.

"Well, we don't look alike? I mean, not really..."

"Of course we do...Why, we share the same eyes, do we not?" she said, and although she smiled, the smile didn't quite reach her eyes.

"Yes," I persisted, "But you are so dark and I so fair..."

"Oh this is nonsense!" she said sharply, and then continued in a softer tone, "Yes...Yes, sorry, my darling, of course you get your colouring from your father..."

I had wanted to pursue the conversation, but I knew to do so would make her angry, and so I dropped the subject. I did, however, notice that she studied me closely over the next few days, and it set me to wondering why my simple questions had upset her so. I suppose I was growing up and I was becoming more and more curious because our conversation that day signalled a change in me also.

I had started to notice things that I had never noticed before, things like the fact that Maman never seemed to eat. She gave the impression of eating and even placed the food in her mouth, but she then would discreetly raise her handkerchief up to her mouth and deposit the food in its folds. I was shocked by this discovery, at first believing that I was simply mistaken, but after watching her several times, I knew that I wasn't. I also noticed that although Maman didn't eat, she did drink, and that she always seemed to have a goblet of red wine in her hand.

The fact that she drank so much started to really concern me, but I knew to confront her would cause yet more angry words, and so instead I chose to avert my eyes when she drank from her goblet.

However, I was starting to get discontented with our way of life. I didn't understand why I was unable to ride without an escort, and even with them, I was only able to ride within the grounds of the chateau. I started to question the fact that we never had visitors, and that we had no friends. I had outgrown my childhood games and no longer dreamed of being a princess, but instead wanted to entertain and discover how other people lived. I was fast becoming a woman, but was still being treated like an over-protected child, and I resented the fact.

Several times I approached Maman and suggested we entertain, but always she would wave her hand in dismissal without even considering what I had to say. One evening, when she had once more waved away my words, I jumped up and flounced out of the room. I was so angry that I didn't bother to respond to her sharp reprimand and command to return to the dining table, and angrily ran up to my bedchamber and flung myself down on my bed where tears of anger and sorrow mingled into huge sobs.

I must have drifted off to sleep, because when I awoke the chateau was in total silence. I was just starting to drift back to sleep when I heard a noise down in the courtyard. The chateau was built around a courtyard; this was in turn surrounded by a very wide and deep moat. I was more than a little curious to discover which one of the servants would be tinkering about in the courtyard in the middle of the night, but there was one thing for certain, whoever it was, was up to mischief.

I quickly pulled on my cloak and ran barefoot down the stairs. I was ready and waiting, lantern lit, and hand on hip, when the cloaked figure pushed open the heavy oak door that led to the courtyard. However, I was more than a little startled when I realised that the person sneaking into the chateau was not the pilfering servant I had been expecting, but instead was Maman. What was even more startling was the fact that she was smothered in dripping blood, which seemed to be everywhere, not just on her clothes, but all over her face and hands.

"Maman!" I cried, running towards her with my arms outstretched, "Oh, Maman...you are injured?"

"STOP!" she growled before I could reach her, her voice both menacing and anguished. "Do not come any closer, Rose. Go to your bedchamber and I will join you shortly." Noticing that I was hesitant to leave her, she shouted, "NOW!"

Although it was not very long before she barged into my bedchamber, to me it felt like many hours had passed.

"Maman!" I said as she entered my bedchamber, relief evident in my voice.

"Do not fret so, Rose, I am fine..." she stated, but her face was a mask, and I was able to see how nervous she was under the facade.

"But...But, what happened?" I asked, puzzled by her reaction to my concern.

"I was out hunting...and the small doe I caught bled out everywhere, including all over me. I am sorry if I scared you...but well, you should have been asleep."

"Hunting...at night, Maman?" I asked, disbelief evident in my voice. She replied, her voice sharp, "Yes, Rose, hunting...now go to sleep!"

She arose from the bed and made her way to the door. However, something stopped her from passing through it, and she stood with her back towards me, obviously contemplating a thought that was troubling her.

"Rose, I believe you are correct about the fact that we need to entertain more..." she said, as she turned back towards me. "It seems to me that I too must be restless. After all, what other explanation is there for my need to hunt at night? None, other than I am bored and that I am in need of a way to alleviate that boredom! From tomorrow we shall remedy the situation."

I was stunned by her sudden change of heart. However, she kept to her promise, and the very next day we started to plan and make preparations for a banquet for the neighbours surrounding Chateau Cadeau. Within weeks, Pierre, my tutor was appointed, and I was instructed to write in this journal. Nevertheless, no matter how excited I was by the changes in my life, I was still not convinced by Maman's explanation of why she was dripping with blood, and that being the case—I was determined to discover the real reason.

Chapter Three

I am so excited, for tonight is the night of our first ever banquet. The chateau is alive with servants, and tradesmen, running to and fro—their quick chatter echoing throughout the long corridors. Now and then I hear a burst of laughter from one of the serving girls, and it's a sound of happiness, a sound I have rarely heard before.

Maman says I should rest, but I am unable to. Instead, I want to watch the men and women transform the great hall into the magical ocean scene Maman has planned. Maman adores the ocean, and after Pierre had told us the tale of the Greek god Poseidon, and his great kingdom of Atlantis, she was so enamoured of the story that she decided the great hall, where the banquet was to be held, would be decorated to resemble the great kingdom, and all attending would dress appropriately.

Oh what fun we have had choosing the materials for our costumes, and for decorating the great hall! I am to be dressed in a gown of the most beautiful pale blue silk, it covers my skirt in layers of many fish scale-like shapes, and when the light reflects, it shimmers, just like a freshly caught fish.

Maman's gown is similar, but of a darker blue colour, and it too reflects with glorious greens and blues. Maman decided that we would forgo the usual ruffled collar, made so fashionable by the good Queen Bess. And instead our gowns are both low cut across the bust, a style that is really quite daring—both creations are exquisitely beautiful. The hall is decorated with length after length of blue and white silk, arranged to resemble waves rolling and crashing. And for our ocean's seaweed there are huge arrangements of ferns and greenery. After much debate, we decided that the feast will consist of only fish dishes, but they are truly delicious dishes, and cook has surpassed herself. We have huge platters of oysters, crab, and lobster, huge golden crust pies and platters of fish in the most perfect sauces. However, more than this I am looking forward to eating the sugar fish sculpture that Maman ordered from the sugar crafter. I have been tempted to break a little of the tail off just to taste the glorious sweetness on my tongue. Alas, it seems Maman has warned the servants that I may try to do this, because every time I approach this glorious creation, someone comes along to shoo me away.

A little earlier I crept into the hall to see how the multitude of servants were progressing, and I was astounded by the beauty that surrounded me. Every part of the hall glittered with candlelight which highlighted the material in such a way that it seemed that the hall was, indeed, submerged into the ocean. The illusion, I am sure, will be talked about all over France, and I am so excited by the fact.

"Rose! We have been looking everywhere for you...you must get dressed!" Maman's voice rang out behind me, causing me to jump and shriek in surprise.
"Maman..." I gasped, "You frightened me..."
"Indeed...well you must hurry..." she answered, but I saw the shadow of a smile lift the corners of her mouth, and I knew that she was amused rather than angry. This being the case, I felt a little more confident and offered a smile towards my nurse, Jeanne, but she didn't smile in return, and so I turned my back on her and snuggled into Maman's side for comfort. Jeanne has been my nurse since the day I was born, and although she loves me dearly, her first love is Maman, and always will be—she adores her.

"It is so beautiful, Maman...." I breathed.

"Yes it is..." Maman replied. Glancing towards her I noticed that instead of feeling happy about the fact, she seemed angry.

"Maman! What's the matter?" I asked her, concern catching my voice.

"Oh nothing, nothing is the matter, my love...but maybe, just...a little too beautiful..." she answered, her voice growing quiet. I was confused by her answer, and said, "But, Maman...how can it be too beautiful...I don't understand?"

"No, of course you don't...and I am being silly..." she said as she slapped my behind and turned me towards Jeanne. Nevertheless, her jaunty smile didn't fool me, and I could see that she was still concerned, but before I could comment she said, "Now, Rose, no more dallying...see how poor Jeanne waits...you must be ready to receive our guests, as must I! No more delays..." I placed my hand in Jeanne's and followed her, but not before I glanced back at Maman and quickly poked my tongue out at her. Her laughter rang out throughout the hall, and I smiled, because I knew that this time her gaiety was real.

Chapter Four

Our banquet was wonderful. I shall never, not for as long as I live, forget it. Everything was so bewildering, but at the same time so enchanting, and there were so many people that I fear I shall never remember all of their names. I will, however, remember how beautiful the women looked in their costumes, and how elegant and handsome the men were as they bowed over my hand in greeting.

I believe I shone, but Maman—Maman glittered. Nonetheless, I felt quite sorry for her, for she was plagued all night by would-be suitors, and it was obvious from the scowl on her face that she was far from amused by their attention. I am ashamed to admit, that I didn't rescue her. I was too intent on remembering every part of the magic, and I ate, drank, laughed, and danced in abandonment.

I was introduced to two young girls from our neighbouring estate which was owned by the Comte Pierre La Fontaine. The first girl, the Lady Marie La Fontaine, was his eldest daughter. And I believe that it would be difficult to find a more ugly or pompous young woman in the whole of France.

She told me she was fifteen years old, but by the way she carried herself, and the way she looked down her ugly long nose at all and sundry, you would think she was an old maid. And I would have taken great delight in telling her so, if I hadn't remembered my manners and risen above her snide and nasty remarks. Not least because I didn't want Maman to discover my rudeness and decide entertaining wasn't for us. However, her sister Colette, who was but a few months older than me, was her complete opposite. She was pretty, with curling dark red hair and bewitching green eyes, and she was vivacious and amusing, and we became instant friends

It was Colette who introduced me to many of our visitors and kept me amused with gossip about each and every one of them when their backs were turned. I laughed until my sides hurt, although the pain, of course, could also have had something to do with the copious amounts of delicious food I had consumed. I was wiping my eyes, after yet another scandalous tale, and was trying desperately to compose myself, when Colette sat forwards, her stare intent on a man who had just entered the hall.

"Oh, but how perfect he is..." she said in a whisper.

My gaze followed her stare, and I must admit that he was indeed perfect. He was very tall—probably the tallest man in the room, but that was only one of the many attributes that made him stand out from the crowd—for he was quite literally beautiful. I know that sounds a little strange when referring to a man, but there is no other way to describe him. His hair was midnight black, his skin dark and swarthy, and his features were, even from the distance far across the hall, well, they were arresting in their perfection and beauty. However, it wasn't just his looks that held one astounded, it was also the overwhelming portrayal of arrogance and power which radiated from him. And his immaculate apparel, which when combined with his arresting looks, well the whole effect seemed to hold one spellbound in admiration. It was apparent from the way he was dressed, in a rich gold doublet encrusted with small gems, that he was also very affluent.

"Who is he?" I whispered in awe.
"Oh la la...he is the guest of the widow of the Vicomte Armand Belliveau, Aimée...see, she stands beside him," she said, nodding towards a small and somewhat shabby looking woman.
"It is said that he is her lover...but I cannot believe it.

I mean, look at her...it does not seem possible, does it? His name is Farand Montague...and it is said that he from a common family...but oh la la...oui, I see that you agree with me?"

"Oui..." I replied, my voice not much above a whisper. I turned towards Marie and was surprised that she too was staring at Monsieur Montague, a rapt expression clearly evident on her ugly face, and I felt a giggle rise into my throat. It seemed that the lady Marie wasn't too proud to find the Monsieur attractive.

"Look!" Colette said, "He is yet another that has spied your maman..." Looking back towards Monsieur Montague, I felt a sudden surge of jealousy rack my body, a feeling which was up until that moment alien to me. Monsieur Montague was indeed striding towards my maman, the poor Vicomtesse trailing in his wake. I was, at that moment, for the first time ever, annoyed that Maman was so beautiful. I wanted me to be the one that that handsome man approached with a look of wonder on his face, and no one else, especially Maman. I turned sharply away from the scene, not wanting to see Maman rebuke him in disdain—like she had all the others. For I felt that he was far above such reprimands, and Maman or any woman should feel honoured to be approached by such a man.

"Oh, Rose...what is the matter?" Colette asked me, with obvious concern.

"Nothing...really I am fine...but, well, maybe I have indulged too much...I feel a little sick," I replied, but I was lying. I did not feel sick, I was angry. I could feel my cheeks flaming and I felt very confused. I have never felt such emotions, for my belly felt like it was spinning, and I felt like the world had come to an end and I had lost everything I held dear.

How bizarre is it that I should feel this way about a man whom I have never seen or even heard of before, and once more I glanced back towards him and Maman, and once more I felt supremely jealous. I could not believe it. Maman, who had spurned every man's advances all night, was now laughing gaily with this man— her new would-be suitor.

"I am very sorry, Colette, Marie," I said, "But I am feeling most unwell...I think I should rest for a little while...please excuse me and hopefully I will see you a little later..." and swiftly turned, without waiting for their response. I then made my way out of the hall and up to my bedchamber—all the while tears streaming down my face.

On reaching my bedchamber, I quickly dried my eyes and patted my still burning face with a cooling wet rag that I had dipped into my wash bowl. I then fell back onto my bed, and placed the rag over my aching eyes, trying, without much success, to stem the flow of tears.

I have, since the event which happened earlier this evening, realised something quite significant—I am in love! I can find no other explanation for my behaviour, and although it seems really quite strange that I can look across a crowded room and know that I have found the man that I will love for all time—I know that it is so.

Once my tears had stilled, and I was feeling composed, I arose. One thing I am not, or have ever been, is a coward, and I knew that I could not stay in my room all night. Not least because Maman would surely miss me and more importantly because I wanted, once again, to look upon the face of Monsieur Montague.

Slowly, I made my way down the winding stairs which led me to the great hall. I placed my slipper-clad feet very carefully for I was still slightly shaky, and I wanted to make sure that I was fully composed before I entered the hall.

I had almost reached the bottom step, when I heard voices from just below me in the entrance to the turret. Not wanting it to seem as if I was eavesdropping on them, and quite hypocritically hoping that I may be able to gather some gossip to share with Colette, I stilled my progress, in the hope that they would soon disappear.

"We are the same, Gwen...surely you are happy that we have found each other...we belong together, my love...it is fate!"
"Don't be so ridiculous!" I heard Maman say with scorn in response to this stranger whom I could not see. "Do you not understand? I hate what I am, if I could change it I would! There is also the fact that we have only just met...no, I wish you to leave, now! I left that part of my life behind, and I have no desire to return to it. You, sir, are not, and never will be, welcome in my home!" I was shocked by the anger vibrating in Maman's voice, for it almost seemed to resonate with a growling quality.
"Oh, my sweet, but it is you who needs to understand! I know already that you burn for me...we both know that these...these, our food! Well, they cannot give you what you want...you want to feel the pure ecstasy in lovemaking that only our kind can share. I know it...and so do you..."

The man's voice, just like Maman's, vibrated with a deep growling quality, and suddenly I was afraid by the sound, and by their words. What did they mean with their words of 'our kind'? It struck me deeply that it was a very strange way to refer to oneself! Quite suddenly, I realised that Maman might be in danger and instantly the anger and jealousy I felt from earlier disappeared, instead my main concern was her safety, and without a second thought, I quickly ran down the remaining few steps.

"Unhand my maman, monsieur," I shouted, "Before I call the gua..." My voice had died in my throat. Monsieur Montague held Maman in a tight embrace, his mouth ravishing hers in an angry kiss of passion, but far from being scared, Maman seemed to be kissing him back just as viciously. What was more bewildering was that when they turned towards me, their faces were not their own, for their eyes had lost all colour. In particular my gaze focused on Maman's eyes, the usual blue part of her eyes was now replaced by a pale colour, similar to the lustre of a pearl, and her pupils were small, but they burnt with a black fire. Monsieur Montague's were the same, but because I was not totally sure of his eye colour I had nothing to compare them too.

"Maman...I do not understand," I heard myself whisper. Maman did not reply, and her head was bowed to her chest. However, when she did look up, I noticed that her eyes had almost returned to normal, and it was then that I realised that she had hidden her face to allow time for her appearance to return to what it was.

"Mademoiselle...I am afraid that you have caught us in the throes of passion...and I apologise. Of course, you are young...and um, well, you do not understand the passion of adults yet, but well, we have an unusual appearance...non?" Monsieur Montague said. He was acting amused, but I could tell from the glare of his almost pitch black eyes, that he was in fact, feeling the opposite.

"It is how Monsieur Montague says, my sweet..." Maman said as she stepped towards me, "I wish you had not seen...but it is done now...come let us return to the hall." Maman spoke gently, and pulled me into her side in an embrace as we walked towards the hall.

I allowed myself to be led and not once did I glance across to Monsieur Montague, who was now casually walking beside Maman on her other side. However, I was not convinced by their explanation. I had seen some of the servants kissing, unbeknown to them, and I had never seen their gaze, no matter how passionate, resemble anything like what I had just witnessed. And as I sit here and recall the event—I am convinced that something sinister is going on, and what is more—I intend, by every way possible, to find out what they are hiding.

Chapter Five

Today we had a visitor. Farand Montague rode into our courtyard, every bit as handsome and arrogant as I remembered him from the banquet. I was alone in my bedchamber, daydreaming about Farand, which was a common occurrence since that eventful night. In fact, I seemed to be filled with misery and confusion all of the time since that night, but I believe that my misery was due, in part, to the sight of Farand's kiss with Maman, and the horror of their faces when I approached them. Maman also seemed to be withdrawn and morose since the banquet, and I had a feeling that her thoughts were very similar to my own.

I was working on my tapestry, a pastime I had in the past hated, but lately it had been a blessed relief and helped me concentrate on something other than my confusing thoughts. I had pricked my finger, and I was not only cursing, but was also sucking on it, in an attempt to ease the pain. I heard shouting down in the courtyard. The chateau was normally so quiet that even someone shouting was an unusual event, and so I made my way to the window to see what was causing such activity.

Farand Montague sat on top of a large chestnut horse, the likes of which is hard to find, being well muscled and startling beautiful. The horse pawed at the ground, half reared, and was snorting in arrogance. The thought crossed my mind that in his arrogance, he suited his owner well.

For the first time in weeks I felt a surge of excitement flow through my body, and without a second thought I pulled on my cloak and made my way down to the courtyard. However, when I burst into the courtyard, I was deprived of the hope that I would be the first one to greet him, because Maman stood by the head of his mount—an intense look of anger on her face. I walked slowly towards them, the need for haste having now passed.

"Aww, and what do we have here? Well, I do believe that it is Mademoiselle Rose, is it not? I have been trying to persuade your maman to come to a feast we are holding tomorrow evening at the Chateau Belliveau, but your maman has declined the invitation...mayhap you will be able to persuade her..." he said, his voice full of charm. The intensity of his gaze caused my skin to colour slightly. And I felt ridiculously happy by the small amount of attention he bestowed on me.

"Can we, Maman?" I said turning towards her, ignoring the thunderous look etched deep into her face.

"I don't think so, Rose...we don't have gowns prepared..." she said, dismissing me and turning back towards Farand, with a triumphant smile showing on her face. However I wasn't going to give up that easily, for suddenly I wanted to visit Chateau Belliveau more than anything in the world.

"But, Maman, we have so many gowns...why I have so many that I have never even worn all of them...as do you...please, Maman!"

"Ah...see, madame...you have no argument! It is only polite, is it not, young mademoiselle...?" he said, looking towards me, "You must attend, madame..." He smiled towards Maman.

Maman looked towards Farand; the expression on her face was that of one with a broken heart. And it suddenly struck me that she was the keeper of many secrets—they were hidden in the depths of her eyes.

"It seems I have no choice in the matter, monsieur..." Maman said, irritation evident in her tone of voice.

"Well in that case I shall see you both tomorrow...good day to you, ladies..." he said, inclining his head. He then turned and galloped his horse out of the courtyard, disappearing almost as rapidly as he arrived.

"Oh thank you, Maman!" I shouted, flinging myself into her arms, and although she embraced me back, she felt stiff and unresponsive.
"We shall need to prepare ourselves...go and find Jeanne and ask her to help you choose a gown...I have a headache and shall lie down for a while."

In the end I chose a white gown embroidered with gold thread and tiny seed pearls. Most of my gowns were of varying shades of blue, chosen to complement my eyes, but I knew that Maman would probably wear blue, and I wanted to look different from her. I was correct in my assumption, and Maman chose a blue gown, which I hate to admit, looked stunningly beautiful on her. Still it does not matter, for I go to my bed tonight with excitement pumping through my veins, and it is a far superior emotion compared to the misery of late. Now I will sleep—and my dreams will be filled with Farand.

Chapter Six

I feel my heart is breaking, and now I wish reverently that we did not visit the Chateau Belliveau. We returned from the blasted chateau just over a week ago, and I have not, as yet, ventured outside of my bedchamber. And I have such a malady of the heart that I have only just mustered up the will to write down how I feel. Maman thinks that I am sick, and I am—sick at the sight of her and Farand fawning all over each other! For it is obvious to all, that they are very much in love.

I ask myself over and over again, why him? Of all the men who showed an interest in her, why did she choose the man I love? Of course, she doesn't know how I feel, and I am determined that she never will, but every time I look at them together I feel a sharp pain pierce me just below my heart, and it seems I will never escape it. Ever since the night of the feast they have spent every day together, and although I enjoyed the evening at the Chateau Belliveau and loved spending time with Colette, their constant flirting and closeness spoilt my fun.
It was as if no one else actually existed for them both. I noticed that poor Madame Aimée Belliveau was beside herself, and constantly tried to gain Farand's attention, but alas, her actions were in vain.

Farand did not even bother to make a show of entertaining her, he simply ignored her, and for the first time ever I felt ashamed of Maman and her lack of manners. I felt that she should have intervened and graciously included Aimée, and I believe I was not the only person who felt this way—I noticed a lot of the older ladies whispering to each other behind their hands after glancing towards Maman. Of course, Maman and Farand did not notice, they did not notice any one other than each other, and I also believe no one else really noticed anyone else but them either. After all, they were the most handsome couple in the room, for they each seemed to glow with an inner light and they were truly a magnificent sight to behold. Especially when they danced La Volta—Farand held Maman with ease, and to watch them was like observing that well known dance for the very first time.

It was at this point that I decided that I had observed enough. I wanted nothing more than to approach them and order Farand to dance with me. Which was, of course, a ridiculous notion. So, instead, I walked out of the hall and made my way into the garden, deciding that I would remain in the trees beside the small lake until I had cooled down and Maman was ready to leave. Ah, but my plan was thwarted.

Farand and Aimée had extended their invitation to us, and it was decided that we would stay for a few days more. I was almost certain that the invitation was not Aimée's idea, as I was sure she would be greatly opposed to the idea—just as I was. However, Maman ignored my request to leave, much the same, as I imagine, Farand ignored Aimée's.

The next few days were like living in a never-ending nightmare. Their constant chatter and laughter could be heard throughout the chateau, and every time a little of their happiness was glimpsed or heard it was like a whip issuing punishing lashes. They never seemed to tire of each other or run out of energy, and they constantly were out hunting on horseback or walking for miles with Farand's eagle, following his flight path, and collecting his prey from his grasp.

It was on third day of our visit that Aimée broached the subject of Maman and Farand's relationship with me. I was resting in a small salon situated on the first floor which overlooked the courtyard. I had heard the sound of Maman and Farand returning from the hunt, their voices were carefree and full of happiness, and although I knew that to walk to the window and peer outside would only serve to cause me pain—it seems that I am a glutton for punishment, for I could not stop myself. I do not know how long I watched, and I did not realise that tears fell unguarded from under my lashes, until Aimée touched my shoulder, her hand soft and gentle.

"Aww, Rose...pray do not cry, my sweet," she said, "There is nothing we can do but look on and weep...they are meant for one and other...you must accept this..."
"I cannot..." I sobbed, falling into her welcoming embrace.
"Yes you will, my sweet...your maman does not know how you feel...non?" I shook my head in response. "That is how it should be...do not tell her, for you are young, my sweet...your prince will come along soon, but Farand...he is...he is not for you."
"But how do you know that?" I said exasperated, "And what about you? I know you love him?"
"Oui...it is so, but I always knew it would be fleeting...I was never, nor ever could be the woman for him...I took what I could when I could...and my memories will last a lifetime."

Suddenly she looked sad, and very, very, old. "But look at him, my sweet, his heart, it is gone...and he will never love another...but you, you will love many...this I promise you. Why, when I was your age I was infatuated by many...and so it will be with you..."

She continued talking, but I had ceased to listen. She was wrong—I knew she was, and be it one year or twenty, I would find a way to make Farand love me and me alone. After all, Maman was old—oh I know she didn't look aged, but she was, and one day her the passing years would catch up with her. I did not doubt this. And when that day came, I would be waiting—a young and beautiful woman whom Farand would fall deeply in love with. And I know that when that day comes it will hurt Maman, but I cease to care. My love for Farand is just too strong, and I will let no one get in the way of that love—not even Maman.

Chapter Seven

Autumn 1575

A whole year has passed since I last wrote, and much has happened in that year. Life within the chateau remains the same, and once more we have ceased to entertain. However, I do not mind, for I find Maman and Farand's displays of affection somewhat embarrassing, and this feeling is, thankfully, slightly diminished with the absence of others.

Farand has now taken up residence in the chateau, and it is his intrusion that has caused the change in Maman and me. We no longer sit and converse because Farand is always present—sometimes it feels like he stalks us and is afraid for us to be alone. Whenever I seek a private audience with Maman, he cuts in, thus making it impossible to dismiss him. Why, only last week I asked Maman if we could talk privately, and before she could reply Farand said, "Oh come, Rose, whatever needs to be said can be said in front of me..."
"But, it is a private matter that I wish to discuss with Maman alone, sir..." I replied, anger, I believe, evident in my stance and manner.

"Well, if it is the fact that you have started your courses, we already know...and we are pleased that you are becoming a woman."

"But...how do you know?" I asked, embarrassment and confusion replacing my anger.

"Jeanne mentioned it," Maman said quickly, casting a flashing look of anger in Farand's direction.

"Maman...please, you must see that I do not wish to discuss this in front of Farand!" Maman stood up from her chair and drew me into her arms. "Yes of course....and I am angry at Farand for mentioning so delicate a subject...but still it is done now...and cannot be undone...so let us forget it for now and we will discuss it later."

However, we didn't discuss it later. Instead Jeanne instructed me on how I must fold a rag and place it in between my legs in order to soak up the blood, but no matter how much I loved Jeanne, I still felt that it was Maman's place to talk to me about this important change in my life. And by the way her mouth twisted in disapproval when she glanced at Maman and Farand—Jeanne agreed with me.

Occurrences like this one were commonplace, and although Maman would be angry with Farand when events like these took place, her wrath seemed to pass quickly and within moments she would once more be loving towards him, and conveniently forget about me.

I believe it is because of events like this that I now feel differently towards Farand, for I no longer love him, but instead, I feel as if I hate him with a passion. It is my opinion that Maman senses how I feel, but she chooses to ignore my feelings, and because of this I feel anger and resentment, directed at both of them, flow through my body like never before.

I know that it is ridiculous, but I have even taken to planning Farand's murder. And although I know that it is only a fantasy, it is a daydream that helps me escape my hatred of him—sometimes I dream for hours of how I will dismiss him from our lives. I especially feel this way when I watch them gallop out of the courtyard from my bedchamber window—I know that they are once more going on one of their many hunting expeditions, and that I, as usual, am not invited and am not welcome.

I believe it was due to their complete indifference towards me that I started to ride alone, for it was just after witnessing their departure in the early days of their relationship, that I decided for the first time that I would do so. On this day my anger was such that I ripped my gown off, and then pulled my riding habit on, ripping it in haste. I then ran towards the stables, still so very angry, and not even bothering to call a groom, I tacked up Belle, my horse.

"What are you doing, mademoiselle? You must wait and I will ride with you," the stable lad, Jean, called out to me.

"No! I wish to ride alone...and if you tell Maman, I will...well, I will tell her you assaulted me...and make it known throughout the chateau that I will do the same to whoever informs her. You know as well as I, that she will have your guts for garters if she was to hear such a tale...do you understand me, boy?"

"Oui, of course, mademoiselle..." he answered, his voice little more than a whisper. Satisfied that he would cherish my secret, I rode hell for leather out of the courtyard, and for the first time—in a very long time—I felt truly alive.

I did not catch up to them on that day, nor on the numerous other occasions I set out in pursuit of them.

However, the fantasy fuelled my mind and body, and I was at last leaving behind my depression and once more enjoying life. That was until the disastrous day that I did manage to catch up with them—a day I wished afterwards had never happened.

You see, I had long ago given up the idea of discovering where they went, but I still loved to ride on my own. I loved the daydreams I conjured on my adventures, and although sometimes they still revolved around Maman and Farand, I had also started to dream of meeting a stranger—a man that I would fall in love with, and who would ultimately become my husband. I also loved to jump fallen trees and hedges, a thrill I would not be allowed to accomplish if I was accompanied by a groom.

It was on a day such as this, when I had spent several hours living in my daydreams, and had jumped and galloped to my heart's content, that I decided to tie Belle to a tree, which was another habit I had taken to, and rest beneath the shade of its branches. I had been lazily dozing, still in the midst of my fantasy, when I heard a growling sound from within the wood behind me.

Of course, I should have quickly untied Belle and ridden away, but for some unknown reason, I felt drawn to the wood and the need to investigate.

Slowly I crept towards the densely wooded area, and although I was afraid, I felt compelled to continue and face the monsters within. I shall never forget the moment I saw them, for I felt bile rise and sting my throat in disgust at what I saw. Maman and Farand, were both naked under the shade of a tree, but this fact alone did not shock me. However, the fact that they held a young peasant girl in between them, and that they held their bloodsoaked mouths to her wrists and throat did.

Fear spiralled throughout my body and I started to breathe in fast but shallow breaths—I then became instantly afraid that they would hear my breathing. My heart was pounding like a drum, and I knew I needed to return to Belle. The last thing I wanted was them to hear or sense my fear and discover my whereabouts.

I shall never know how I managed to walk with stealth back to my horse. Nor how I managed to ride home to the chateau and make my way to my bedchamber without passing out or vomiting—but I did.

I fell onto my bed in relief, and once the shock of what I had seen had worn off, I started to piece together that which I had seen. It wasn't l0ng before I came up with the logical conclusion—and that conclusion was that Maman and Farand were vampires!

Chapter Eight

I am, for the first time in my entire life, afraid of Maman. Of course, now that I can look back with my newfound knowledge, I realise the reasons why she never ate food, there was a lack of entertaining, and why the pair of them frequently ventured on their hunting expeditions without inviting me along. Everything, for the first time, made total sense—but how I wish it didn't! I wanted us to be normal, but now I realise that we never shall be. However, more than this, I feel disgust. I am truly disgusted that Maman preys on the weak—sucking the life from her victims to enable her to survive—it is a sickening thought, and one that is abhorrent to me.

I don't know how I made it through dinner that evening, but for once I was thankful that they took little notice of me and conversed amongst themselves. Shortly after the meal had been cleared away, I excused myself on the pretext that I had a headache, and quickly escaped to my bedchamber. Well, almost. I had just reached my door when I felt a hand grab my shoulder, and with a startled gasp I spun around to find Farand's handsome face staring at me.

"You startled me....what do you want?" I snapped.

"Oh dear, I am sorry, Rose...I did not mean to scare you..." he said, an amused smile hovering on his lips. He paused for a moment, expecting, I think, for me to comment. He must have grown weary of waiting for my response because finally he said, "I hear you have taken to riding alone of late?"

"Who told you that?" I barked, but inside I had started to feel sick, and fear crept inside of me, and like a disease it rendered me helpless, turning my bones to liquid.

"Oh...well, shall we say a little bird...um, hiding in a tree...or perhaps behind...yes behind a tree is a better description." His eyes took on the opaque glimmer that I had witnessed the first night we had met, when I had interrupted his passionate embrace with Maman, and I felt my legs grow weaker.

"Well...you are mistaken, sir," I said, turning away from him towards my bedchamber. Again, he grabbed my arm and spun me back towards him.

"Non, I do not think so, mademoiselle. I saw you...and I know you watched us...and now we must do something about it...explanations are in order, I think."

"Well, I wish Maman to explain everything to me...not you!" I said, ripping my arm from his grasp.

"Mmmm, but Maman does not know you were there, and it would distress her to know that you were. I think it is better if we keep this between ourselves...a secret. Oui, a secret. Nonetheless, I still need to discuss this matter with you...I will meet you alone tomorrow in the cellar...at um, midday...do you agree?"

"Why the cellar?" I asked him, curious to why he had decided on that particular location when I was sure it would have been more secure to meet outside of the chateau.

"Gwen never ventures there...and I do not want her to overhear what I want to talk to you about...so, I will see you there?" I wanted to hear his explanation, but I was terrified at the thought of being alone with him, so I said in a whisper, "I do not wish to die..."

"Ah...but I do not wish to kill you, my little bird...if I did, well, you would be dead by now. Non, I just wish to speak with you...so, my little bird, will you meet me tomorrow?" He asked me in a soft, almost caressing, voice, and placing his finger under my chin, which had fallen to my chest, he lifted my face up so that he could look into my eyes.

"I will never hurt you, my little bird...I promise..." Suddenly, it was as if I was transported back to the very first time I saw him.

The love I felt for him then resurfaced, and my heart quickened under his intense gaze.

"Do you believe me?" he asked me, his voice soft and tender.

"Yes..." I heard myself reply to his question, but it was as if I was in a beautiful dream, and he seemed so far away, but, yet, so near. Swiftly, he bent his head to mine and kissed my lips. However, it wasn't a kiss of passion, but a chaste, almost sweet kiss. The feelings it evoked caused my heart to beat a rapid rhythm, and my legs to grow so weak that they threatened to fail my body. My head had once more fallen to my chest, and when I regained my composure, I lifted it to once more gaze into his beautiful eyes, but he had disappeared.

I walked into my bedchamber, my heart was in a whirl, but my head was surprisingly clear, and in contentment I sunk back onto my bed to dream. Strangely, I seemed to be able to accept the fact that Farand was a vampire, much more so than I could accept the fact that Maman was. I wondered why? Why was I willing to forgive in him, that which I was unable to forgive in Maman? The answer came to me quickly—Maman had betrayed my trust.

She had lied to me for years, and still did, for I knew deep down that she would never impart her secret to me. And to me at least, our years together had been nothing but a tangled web of betrayal, and above this I felt as if the woman that was my Maman—was not only a stranger to me—but also a monster.

Chapter Nine

I was so nervous the next day that even Jeanne commented on my behaviour, stating that she was sure that I had consumed a morsel of food that had not agreed with me. I didn't contradict her, not only would it have been a wasted exercise, because once Jeanne's mind was made up, there was no changing it, but also because I wished her to believe her own theory.

I waited, not so patiently, for midday to approach, and when it was almost time, and I could stand the waiting no longer, I ran with gusto down into the cold and damp cellar. I had rarely ventured into the dark empty space before, not only because Maman expressly forbade me to trespass there, but because it was creepy and smelled of mildew and decay. Therefore, I was relieved that Farand was waiting, and presented himself as soon as I entered.

"Rose..." he said, stepping forward out of the shadows.
"Hello, Farand," I said, sounding a lot more confident than I felt. "So I am here...what do you wish to discuss with me?"
"Aww, mademoiselle...you sound so cold and distant...we are friends, are we not?"

"Yyes...wwe are..." I stammered, all at once feeling nervous and shy.

"Good...first of all I wish you to know that you have nothing to fear from me, Rose. I am your friend, a true friend...do you understand?" I nodded in response to his question—afraid to speak for fear of blurting out my true feelings for him.

"I know you saw your maman and me, and I believe you have guessed that which is our true nature...am I correct, Rose?"

I turned away from him, once more feeling fear rush through my veins.

"Do not fear me, Rose, tell me...please..."

"I bbelieve that you are...tthat you are...vampires..." I stammered, my voice ending in a whispered sob that vibrated in my throat. Suddenly, I felt myself being lifted into the air and Farand's arms turning me so that I was snuggled into his chest, and I stayed there, crying and sobbing, as Farand told me the truth about my birth, my family, and my life.

After a while my sobbing ceased, and I listened—really listened, and my anger towards Maman burned inside of me. She had changed the course of my life with her lies and betrayal—betrayal of not just me but many. And in those few moments my love for her deserted me in a misty, cold black hate—an emotion so powerful that I wasn't sure it would ever leave me.

Chapter Ten

It's been a long time since I have shared my thoughts and feelings, and even now, I find it difficult to express the words to describe my heartbreak and despair. My whole life has been a lie. I can find no simpler way to voice how I feel about the tale Farand told me on that fateful day I agreed to meet him in the cellar.

Maman lied to me about almost everything. Well, I call her Maman, but it seems that she is not even what she claims to be, for she is my *grand-mère*, and my true maman still lives in England. What is more, I have a twin brother and a father who lives. Farand told me all about them as I wept in his arms, and so detailed was his description that I almost feel like I know them personally. Of course, for the moment I can only but dream, and no matter how I fantasise about knowing them, it is just that—a fantasy. However, I have made up my mind that I will travel to England, and I will take up my rightful place beside my family.

Oh, I know this is a dangerous course to take, for Farand told me everything, and it seems that I was to be sacrificed at my father's rebirthing ceremony and my blood was to be his first as a vampire.

However, Maman snatched me before the ceremony was completed, and in doing so she murdered Matilda, my father's adopted mother. Robert Vanike, my *grand-père,* and the leader of all vampires, was beside himself with rage, and so Maman fled to France, knowing that he would kill us both in an instant. However, it seems that my grand-père had a change of heart and he sent Farand to France to find me so that in time he might impart to me the truth, and after doing so, return me to my family.

How I wish it was that simple—for no matter how much I wish to return to them, I could not, at the time, leave Maman. I hated her for a while, but now I realise that I love her, and I always will, and although she lied to me, I know she had her reasons and she was protecting me—with her life if need be. I just wish she had told me the truth from the outset, for I feel that if she had, then I wouldn't now be feeling such a deep sense of betrayal. For it seems that no matter how hard I try, and although I think that I am being unreasonable—I am unable to shake this feeling of pain that seems to reside deep within my heart. So, it is only now, almost two years later, that I realise that I must do what Farand urged me to do that day in the cellar—I must leave Maman.

I have puzzled long and hard over my decision, and sometimes I have been so bewildered and confused that I have wanted to run to Maman and ask her advice. However, to do so would have been a useless exercise, for I know that she would have persuaded me that we should flee, and no matter how tempting that course of action would be, I knew then, and I know now, that it would be the wrong decision. So, not once have I confided in Maman. She does not even know that I know that she is a vampire, and that is how it should be, for this decision, for the first time in my life, should be mine and mine alone.

I have spent many months, days and nights, and so many tears, trying to figure out what I should do, and now, at last, I feel a sense of relief that I have reached my decision. I have endured Farand's impatience and anger, and my own, but it is with conviction that I start the next phase of my life.

This phase, I believe, will involve my rebirth into a vampire, and might place my whole being in jeopardy. You see, I know that there is a chance that Farand may be lying, and that he is simply returning the fatted calf to its destiny, and that my family may still sacrifice my life—just like they planned to do so many years ago.

However, it is a gamble that I am willing to take, and if my destiny is to be a sacrifice, then so be it, for I am at last prepared for that eventuality.

I feel so tired, but then I tire so easily since my discovery. Two years is a long time to feel fatigued and besieged by questions that my poor muddled mind can barely find the answers to. It is my hope that the malady that invades my mind will recede and allow me, once more, to live in freedom of thought.

My malady has caused such anguish in the chateau over the last few months, and Maman, being afraid for my sanity, has summoned many of the best physicians. Nevertheless, their remedies never work, after all—how could they? I can confide in none of the knowledge that threatens my mind.

If anything, their treatments have weakened me. For the sight of leeches sucking my blood, and according to the physicians, the bad humours from my body, is nothing short of grotesque. Even more so, since witnessing Farand pop the bulbous blood-bloated monstrosities into his mouth, whilst declaring, "Ah, they are but delicious morsels of nectar, my love!"

The sight of him chewing and savouring the leeches is disgusting to say the least—and an act I would wish no other human being to see.

I have felt my sanity come dangerously close to breaking after witnessing moments like this. And sometimes I feel that I have given in to the temptation of madness, especially when I float in a world of my own. I remain this way for many days—in a dreamlike state. I am surrounded by images of Maman and Farand in the woods, of blood and gore, and the sight of my own body lying prone and lifeless on my bed. However, I am always able to escape these images, and after days of roaming lost in the fog of my own mind—I return to reality, albeit angry and deranged. It is at these times that I lose my temper, and I throw anything I can lay my hands on at whoever enters my bedchamber. After these outbursts, I have watched the physicians huddled together whispering, and it is their words of, "Insane, and, mad!" that have finally enabled me to make my decision.

I feel now that I must retire, for the mist starts to descend, and I must not succumb to its power. I have no time for it—for tomorrow I start my journey to England.

Chapter Eleven

So these are my last hours within the walls of the chateau. I will not be taking my journal, for I believe that it is part of my past and that I must leave it behind if I am to truly embrace my future. Of course, I shall miss writing, because in a strange and beautiful way I feel that the leaves of this book have become my secret friend and confidante. Which is a ridiculous statement, but it is one that, nevertheless, sums up how I feel. It holds all of my secrets and it is a part of me, and I leave it behind with a sense of sadness. It is, however, a sadness born of a person who in fact never existed, a girl whose life was but a dream—a life concocted from her maman's imagination—a girl who should have died a long time ago.

I am to meet Farand shortly in the woods just beyond the chateau walls, and from there we will ride with haste towards a secret mooring and a ship that will ferry us to England. I am no longer afraid or confused, and I rejoice in the fact that within a few short weeks I will rejoin the family I have never known. I do not know what adventures await me, but I am excited by the thought that I will no doubt participate in many.

You see, from now on I mean to embrace life with abandonment and vigour, and I have decided that never again will I live my life as if I am a strolling player practising for a scene.

Maman, I write this for you, for I know that you will be reading my words. I hope you understand what I have written, and I hope that you leave me to follow my own destiny, for my words above truly convey to you how I feel. I also know that you would never have allowed me to follow this course if I had confided in you, and so I hope you forgive me for leaving you without saying goodbye. I will miss you so much, and although I admit that I have hated you, please be assured that I have always loved you, and will continue to always do so.

I am sure we will meet again. After all, if I am allowed to live, then it is a certainty that we shall both live very long lives. So with this in mind, I beg of you, my sweetest Maman, please do not mourn my leaving. I convey to you the fact that I am certain we will embrace again, and it will be as if we never parted, for my heart will remain with you always.

I give this journal into your keeping, for in truth it tells a story that you created, and although it is a work of fiction, it is a tale filled with love, hope, and courage, for this story is yours, Maman—it was never mine.

Until we meet again.

Rose.

Part 3

Chapter Twelve

Gwen
The lost years

The day Rose left was the day I stopped living. I survived, I existed, but that was all, for all the joy and love I had held so dear to my heart was gone, and with the demise of these precious emotions went that one little part of my soul that had remained. I wept, screamed, and then I murdered and maimed innocent people, but it was all to no avail, for there was nothing I could do to stop the pain, and so finally after many months—I sat.

I sat and I devoured Rose's journal. I read it over and over, until I knew the words off by heart, but the yearnings, secrets, and pain of her soul did nothing to console me. Instead I saw myself as she saw me, and it was a terrifying image of aloofness, selfishness, and pure arrogance. A woman so obsessed with her own desires and her own beauty that she ignored all that she held dear, because there was no doubt that I had ignored Rose.

I let Farand worm his way into our lives with his flattery and proclamations of love, because deep down I was so arrogant that I believed that all men found me to be irresistible—what a fool I was. It had never even entered my head that he might have been lying to me so that he could get closer to Rose. The ironic aspect of this scenario is that Robert knew—he knew how to get past my defences. He knew that I would be susceptible to Farand's flattery, and that I was so selfish that I would believe that he was deeply in love with me, my pride and vanity ensuring that it would be a question I would never ask of myself—let alone Farand. He had known me better than I knew myself, and he had guessed that I was shallow enough to ignore my darling girl's needs. And in doing so, he knew it would make her vulnerable to the fact that she believed that she had a loving family waiting for her across the English Channel.

The knowledge that Robert had so easily duped me into losing my precious girl ate away at me. After all, how could I ever hope to defeat him when I did not even know my own failings, and so I sat and searched the foolish and self-indulgent soul I had lost.

I looked back at my life, at the days when I was but a small child. I remembered my mother's smile and gentle hands, and I wept, for I had walked away from her so easily and not once did I look back. Of course, Robert witnessed me abandon them. He also watched me walk away from Tom as he swung from the rafters of the barn. Tom, the man I had loved and was to wed, and the man whose child I carried inside of my womb, but more than this—he was the man whom I betrayed by loving the animal that killed him. Was it any surprise that Robert knew how selfish and self-serving I was? After all he had witnessed a heartless woman walk away from all she held dear, with only a flurry of tears to indicate that she felt anything at all. However, that was the very least of my failings, for he watched as I walked away from his own love and the close proximity of my child, and for what reason? None other than he was not willing to allow me to visit Henry until he was a little older, but, of course, once again that wasn't good enough for me. And so I disobeyed him, and what is more I tried to steal the child I had given up to him. The worst part being that he had never broken his oath, not once, but I had broken my oath so many times. Yet he still let me live, and as I sat wallowing in self-pity I wondered if I would have been so forgiving? I have taken so much from him, his love, his trust, and then I murdered Matilda, and stole Rose in the process, and not once did I consider his feelings. How easy it must have been for Robert to know that I would abandon Rose's love for Farand's; after all, it is all I have ever done—abandon those I love, or more appropriately—those who love me.

The discovery of my own nature assaulted me, stabbing me over and over again, and I remembered something. I remembered how many times I had referred to Robert and Matilda as animals, but it was then that I knew that it was not they who were the animals, but it was me—I was the beast hidden behind sheep's clothing.

It is so difficult to look at oneself and realise that you are not the person, or in my case—vampire, that you always proclaimed yourself to be. I understand now why Matilda was so scathing towards me when I had first entered Vanike Manor. For I am sure that she saw the real me, the person that I, myself, had failed to see. I was such a hypocrite, treating them all like they were no better than animals and looked down on them, believing I was superior.

And all the time I was taking, with open arms, their hospitality, their riches, and their status, which of course, was far above my former lowly self. I had even met King Henry, and still I proclaimed I was better than any one of them and made no secret of the fact that I found their lifestyle abhorrent.

What a silly little fool I was. Acting like a saintly person who sacrificed everything for her son, when in truth, well, I wanted to live for me. I wanted eternal life, riches and above all else—I wanted Robert!

I cringed in shame at how ridiculous I was, and sank lower and lower into a vat of self-pity—hoping for a death that would never come. And if it did, would I embrace it—no I would not. I would sit on my throne of self-importance, and once more I would find an excuse to justify my worthless existence.

Chapter Thirteen

Days, months, and many years, passed by without my notice. I drank from my servants by bewitching them, but over the years their numbers dwindled. Some died, others left my service, but not before they had left the chateau bereft of riches and in doing so ensuring wealth in their future. I didn't care and failed to see them leave, they could have ripped the clothes off my back and I would not have noticed—so lost was I in misery.

Of course, the chateau fell into disrepair without their tending, and it began to crumble around me. The fields were left untended and became overgrown with weeds, the woodlands became wild and unmanageable, and the chateau became aged and decrepit. However, it was all just an extension of my addled and insane mind, and I didn't notice. How could I? I had lost Rose—the reason why I had made the chateau a home in the first place, and with her went the desire to continue my domestication. Instead I read and re-read Rose's journal, and sometimes I could swear I heard her soft lilting voice speaking the words of her thoughts. Then I would smile in delight, and then later— later I would cry, for I would realise that it was just a dream—purely a dream.

My dreams were the only occurrences that gave me hope. I would watch my beautiful girl dance and float in front of me, her softly curling blonde hair blowing gently in the breeze. And I would hear her musical laughter floating around the room—beckoning me to dance and sway to an imagined tune. However, my dreams one day came to an end and I awoke to find myself in stark reality.

It was for me, at first, a day like any other. I sat, as always, in my salon, Rose's journal open upon my lap. I heard the rustling of skirts, but as always I did not look up and I did not acknowledge the entry into my private domain.

"Madame...I...must speak with you..." I heard the words, but I failed to recognise the voice, and so I did not answer.
"Madame...it is important...you must wake up..." For some reason the yearning sound of the old and pathetic voice roused my interest, and I lifted my eyes to survey the wrinkled, but loving face that stared down at me.
"Who are you?" I asked her, my voice croaky from lack of use.
"It is I, Madame...Jeanne..." I was confused. How was it possible? This woman was not Jeanne. Jeanne was young and beautiful, and this woman—this woman was old and aged.

"No...you are not Jeanne...go away, you old hag..." I whispered and started to turn away.

"Madame...please!" the woman begged, tears brimming from her old and weary eyes. "It is truly I...you have...well you have...your mind left you, for so long...but now you must wake for I have nothing to offer you other than my own wrist and throat. You will die once I am gone...and so you must rouse...please, Madame!" My mind peeled back the layers of forgotten years, and all at once I knew the old woman in front of me was indeed Jeanne—for only my trusted servant would sacrifice her own life for mine.

"Jeanne...oh Jeanne..." I sobbed. Jeanne fell to her knees and wept. Her aged face crumpled into either joy or pain, for she was so old that I could not tell which it was. I fell onto the floor beside her and taking her into my arms—I also wept. I wept for everything I had lost, but more than this, I wept for Jeanne. The one person who loved me, and more than loving me, she was willing to sacrifice her life in order for me to live.

"I will never take from you..." I whispered into her ear, "But you must take from me..." Before she had time to protest I bit down into the artery in my wrist, and placed the flowing blood to her lips.

I held her head firmly with my other hand, and forced my wrist into her mouth, thus ensuring that she would swallow my blood. After a moment, when I was sure that she had swallowed enough, I pulled away, and was relieved to see that already the ageing process had started to reverse, and although she was not young, she looked like the woman I knew and loved.

"Why did you do that, Madame?" she said as she wiped my blood from her lips with a look of disgust.
"So that you can heal and live...and now I will give you a choice!"
"A choice?" she whispered hesitantly.
"Yes...I want to ask you if you wish to become as I am, a creature who will never die...or if you wish to drink my blood on occasion and live a very long life, but of course you will die eventually..."
"I...I...could not...would not want to live as you do...I...I..." Her voice timidly tailed off until her mouth opened but no sound was heard. I threw my head back and laughed, startling her in the process.
"So be it..." I shouted, once more pulling her into my embrace, "You have made a good choice, Jeanne...why, if I had the choice I would not want to be this way either...and you can drink a little of my blood in milk...do you agree?"

She dropped her head in agreement, but I could see the idea was distasteful to her. I smiled, and patting her hand said, "You'll get used to it...I promise..." I then walked towards the salon door, paused, and then turning back towards Jeanne said, "Come...we have much to tend to..." I then walked from the room that had been a prison of my own making for forty-nine years.

Chapter Fourteen

Day by day and step by step we healed. Jeanne achieved this by drinking my blood mixed with a little milk. I, however, did so by returning to my roots and I worked day and night to restore the chateau and grounds. As I worked I remembered my mother, father, and brothers, and sometimes the image of them working in the fields beside me was so real that I could swear that I heard their voices rich in laughter. I heard my brothers teasing me about my love for Tom, their young voices innocent and sweet. I recognised my father's gruff voice telling them to hush and get on with their work, and my mother's soft smile as she stood and surveyed the family she loved.

These memories helped me regain part of my lost soul, and I felt an emotion I had not felt for nearly one hundred years—I felt content. Of course, I still thought of Rose often, but gradually the memories were less damning, and instead I found myself remembering the wonderful times we had shared together. These memories calmed me and I started to once again read her journal, but this time I saw the love and concern she felt, and I heard her soft voice tell her story with her emotions, and not my own.

The time I spent within the salon walls, years I would later refer to as the lost years, had changed me. However, they had not changed me for the worse, but for the better, and I sometimes wonder if this was Rose's intention. After all, she was so much wiser than I, for she didn't act on impulse, but thought about her problems and worked through them, and in doing so she found solutions. I had never found solutions for ways to deal with my problems, but Rose had forced me to do so, and although I had descended into madness I had returned with a mind clear of arrogance and a much truer image of who and what I really was.

However, it was not just I who had changed whilst I was lost in the world of my own torment. The world in which I lived had also changed. I first noticed this when I ventured from the chateau to hunt, for I had once again taken to waylaying strangers. However, I no longer left the travellers I apprehended weak and vulnerable, but now stole only a little of their blood, and left them some gold jingling deep in their pockets. Of course, my actions did not justify my theft, but they eased my conscience a little, and made the way I survived seem a little less brutal and self-serving than ever before.

It was whilst out hunting that I noticed that for the majority of the travellers the ruff worn around the neck, made so fashionable by our good queen Bess, had been replaced for men and women alike by a white cotton or lace collar. The men now seemed to be less ornate, and wore dull fabrics with only a slight slash of colour tied around their waists, although the women's clothing remained bright, but now some women wore their neck and shoulders bare. And their hair, they now left to cascade naturally, with small curls adorning the head and side of the face. I liked the new styles and quickly adopted them, for I found them to be less austere and more suited to my face and figure.

However, clothing seemed to be the least important change I had missed, for whilst I wallowed in my madness, England and France had crowned not one, but two new monarchs each. Our good queen Bess had bequeathed her title to the son and heir of her greatest enemy, namely Mary Queen of Scots, and James the First had united Scotland and England under his rule before passing the throne on his death to his son Charles the First.

Nevertheless it seemed that like his father before him, Charles believed that a monarch was ordained by divine right, something that he argued with his ministers about regularly. Thus, it seems that England is in a state of extreme unrest, and many foretell that a civil war will soon be the consequence of the rule of the new king. There is also tell of the rapid growth of Puritanism in the streets of England. Puritans believe in all things godly, and the only way to achieve this godly state is by servitude and constant prayer. Thus, beauty, enjoyment, and anything deemed to be evil is sought out and destroyed. My travellers have told me bloodcurdling tales of death and destruction aimed towards those that the Puritans have branded to be witches or the spawn of the devil. And I am pleased that I no longer live in the country I have always loved so much.

The changes in France have been slightly less dramatic, and the war of religion had ceased with the crowning of Henri the Fourth, and his return to Catholicism. His son Louis the Thirteenth now sits on the throne and is the second king of the Bourbon dynasty. He looks set to remain king, and in doing so secure the throne for his descendants.

I found these changes to be of interest to me, and often Jeanne and I would discuss them at length in the evenings as we sat cosy by the fire. Although, in truth, these events had very little bearing on our lives; and we remained in our bubble of contentment—and what a bubble it was. Rarely in my life, prior and since this time, have I enjoyed such peace and tranquillity. There were so many days that I failed to talk, but instead gloried in the beautiful nature and ever-changing world around me. I marvelled at the small animals I watched frolic in spring and grow in summer, and how the world changed every few months with vivid colours and mesmerising perfection. I noticed the world, and fell in love with it, and in doing so, made myself a promise that I would never take it, or the people I love for granted ever again.

I was starting to become the person that I always believed I was up until Rose departed. I was, maybe for the first time ever, seeing life how it truly was and not via the confused thoughts and silly whims of a young girl. For I believe that is what I was before, but now I had changed into a woman—albeit a vampire woman.

Of course, change is inevitable, and life will, as I have discovered over five centuries, always turn around and topple you from your contentment. Thus, so it was for Jeanne and me, and our little world would soon shatter and falter—and once again our lives would take on a new direction.

Part IV

Chapter Fifteen

1627

Gwen

The day my life changed once again was at first just as peaceful and beautiful as the magical days I have just described. I was working in the kitchen garden, and although I was unable to eat any of the produce I grew, I worked tirelessly so that Jeanne had plenty of fresh food. I also took great delight in sharing what was left over with the poor of Bordeaux, especially the children. Watching their small pinched faces light up when they bit into a sweet juicy apple was reward in itself, and one that I had grown accustomed to.

"Madame...Madame!" I heard Jeanne urgently calling me and smiled. Her voice, as usual, was shrill and panicked, and I imagined that she believed that some disaster was about to descend. However, Jeanne's idea of a disaster was a pan of water boiling over and dampening the stove—so I was not unduly concerned by her screams.

.

"Shhh...what is it, Jeanne?" I said, my voice calm and low.

"Madame...we have visitors....I think you should come..." Her face was ashen, and she looked to be very disturbed.

"Oh my sweet..." I muttered gently, "Why, you look ill....you stay here and I will go and talk to our visitors. Really, Jeanne, you must try to calm yourself down...I'm sure it's just a few wandering travellers...now sit yourself down and I will be right back." To my utter surprise, Jeanne slipped down onto the dirt and wound her arms tightly around my legs.

"Non, non, Madame...we must leave, we must leave now! Please let us depart..."

"Jeanne! Will you please stop this! You are being ridiculous!" I snapped at her, my voice gruff with irritation.

"Madame...it is them...they have found us...they have returned to kill you...oh please, please, let us leave..."

Her words sent a shiver of dread spiralling down my spine, the force of which was so severe that I bent double as if winded by the impact.

"You see, Madame...we must leave..." Jeanne whispered, her voice full of fear.

"No, Jeanne...I must...I must find out what they want with me," I said as I slowly straightened up.

I felt as if I was in a dream and the world had tinged with a red haze—the red being that of my blood as it flowed from my body. I awoke from my stupor as I looked down into her trusting gaze.

"You must hide," I said, ripping her to her feet. "You must hide in the barn where I slaughtered the pig the other day...yes, yes..." I said as I swung in a circle trying to get my mind to engage and think. "You must hide in the barn....they will not be able to detect your scent over the stench of its rotting blood...go wait in the barn and I will come and find you soon...."
"Non...non...I will stay with you, Madame....I will not leave you..."
"YES YOU WILL!" I shouted as I shook her roughly. "You will go and wait and not come out of hiding for anyone else but me...do you understand?" Tears were streaming down her face as she stared at me and I felt my heart soften. "Please tell me you understand, and will do as I say, Jeanne?" I said, my voice now gentle.
"Yes, Madame...I understand," she whispered, her head falling to her chest in defeat and sorrow.
"Good...now run along," I said as I turned towards the chateau.

I waited until Jeanne was out of sight, and then started to walk towards my foe. For I knew it was Robert who awaited me, and I believed this time he would destroy me.

Chapter Sixteen

Strangely enough, once I knew that Jeanne was safe, I was no longer afraid. If today was going to be my last, then so be it, for I had finally come to terms with who I was, and even if being a vampire wasn't ideal— it was what I was and I accepted the fact.

Many other thoughts floated through my mind as I walked towards the chateau— fear, love, regret, but above these I felt relief. I was relieved that I was now able to give up the fight and rest, for I had found peace at last and had come to the conclusion that I would be able to die without any regrets.

As I walked towards the chateau, flashes from my past filled my mind's eye and I saw Henry as a baby and then as a young man. He was the son I had never really known, but even so, I realised that I had always loved him. Then his daughter—my beautiful Rose—the child of my heart, filled my vision. I wished that everything could have been different, however, vampirism was, and had been our destiny, and there was ultimately nothing I could do to change that destiny.

I felt the presence of the visitor as soon as I entered the chateau.

However, I was surprised, for I knew instinctively that it wasn't Robert who waited for me. The intruder's scent was new and slightly sweet, not old with a hint of rich mustiness and the vibrant blood which was that of Robert.

Slowly, I pushed the door of the salon open and without hesitation walked inside to face the intruder. Rose stood tall and proud in front of me, and although she was of slight frame, strength radiated from her in waves.

"Hello, Maman...or should I say grand-mère?" she said, her voice deep and husky. Her tone held no hint of compassion or fear, but instead vibrated with contempt.
"Oh, Rose...Oh my sweet..." I said, starting to step towards her.
"Oh no, please..." she said, holding her hand up in order to stop me coming any closer. "I really do not want any idiotic show of emotion...I am not the girl you once knew, and I have no use for love or compassion..." Her voice hissed with hate and her eyes had taken on an opaque hue. The malice in her stance stopped my progress, not because I was afraid of her, but because I was shocked by her anger.

The vampire in front of me was not my Rose. Oh, she looked like Rose and was as beautiful and elegant in her blonde fragility. Nevertheless, she was not the girl I remembered. In fact, she was not a girl at all—she was the epitome of a scorned and enraged vampire. A vampire, who had obviously become an evil shadow of a former sweet, angelic, woman. And as I stood there looking at her I realised that the girl I had loved had died when the woman had become a vampire.

"What's the matter, Maman? Do you not like what you see in front of you?" she said, a wicked smile twisting her face into something that was truly ugly.

"You have changed," I said in answer to her question, not wanting to give her the satisfaction of knowing how the changes in her crucified me.

"Yes, well, according to Robert, I am one of the few who changes beyond all recognition when transformed into a vampire. He watches me intently...afraid of what I might do next...I am not even permitted to be in the same room as my nephew's child, lest my blood lust becomes too much of a temptation...

which I am afraid is very likely. I love nothing more than the taste of the young and innocent, reminds me of how I was in my youth...and when I take their young lives...it seems that just for a moment...I get revenge for what you did to me, my dearest Maman. However, the feeling never lasts, and so I must take and take in order to satisfy my appetite."

"So I am now a great-great grandmother?" I asked her.
"Oh yes, Maman...Robert insists on all the men producing an heir before they are changed, but alas, Maman, life goes on without you...or should I say in spite of you!" A smirk twisted her face, but I turned away from the evil I witnessed, for I was unable to confront the cruelty I saw there—the cruelty she indicated I had caused. Her high-pitched, almost manic laughter felt like a dagger piercing my heart, and a tear strayed from under my lashes and made its way wearily down my cheek.

"Oh, Maman...have I hurt you?" she said, humour evident in the catch of her voice. Not waiting for my reply she continued, "Robert said my behaviour would punish you. He said that you have compassion, and for you, my blood lust will be far worse than death."

Once again, her manic laughter rang out around the room. The sound vibrated deep in my mind, causing me to silently cry out as I witnessed the slaying of her once beautiful soul.

Turning back towards her, I swallowed down my disgust and pain, and with a voice that was steady and unfeeling said, "Rose, you have had your fun...now perhaps you will be polite enough to tell me the reason why I am honoured with your presence?"

"Why, of course, Maman. I am here to evict you from the chateau and grounds. I wanted to kill you, but alas Robert decided there was no need; my actions, he believes, will punish you enough...I admit I was far from happy, but I concede that he is probably correct."

"You...you...want the chateau?" I asked her, my voice suddenly fragile and unsteady.

"Yes...so, if you would be so kind as to start packing..."

"And if I am not so kind?" I asked her, my voice low.

"Well...then...Maman dearest...you will leave us no other choice other than to kill you."

Chapter Seventeen

"Why?" I asked her, "Why do you need the chateau? And you said 'us', who is here with you?"

"One question at a time, Maman, please," she said walking towards me, her eyes still opaque, shining like chips of diamonds, luminous in their intensity and hatred.

"I am sure that you have heard of the troubles in England...it seems that we are not welcome there anymore...and the witch hunters...well let us just say that they do not like our kind very much."

I sat down heavily on the bench behind me and looked up into Rose's face—she was now standing no more than an arm's length away from me.

"So, let me guess…they have objected to you killing their babies?" I said softly, staring at her, trying, without success to find the soul that had once lived inside of her.

"Yes they have! However, I am not the only murderer am I, Maman? We all kill and take what is not ours to take. Nevertheless, I will admit that I partook a little more than others. Vanike Manor was besieged by the do-gooders, and well, we lost many of our brothers and sisters! Still, what is done is done, and now we must start again...I suggested the chateau to Robert...and here we are."

"So I see," I said sarcastically, "So who does the 'us' include?"

"Robert, my brother and his wife, Catherine, my father and mother...and a few others...none of them have any wish to see you, for they feel they will kill you if they so much as glimpse your face," she said, a twisted smirk once more marring her beauty.

"Do they indeed!" I whispered and then paused. When I continued my voice was soft, but not afraid, "Well they may have need to kill me...for I do not believe I shall leave the chateau until I have talked with Robert at the very least. Then and only then, will I leave...unless, of course, he decides to kill me, in which case I will remain for all time...and just mayhap I will haunt you all for all time."

Suddenly Rose's arm shot out and her hand held my throat in a searing grip. "Do you not think you have haunted me enough, Maman?" she lisped through her protruding fangs, which had grown in length and glistened brilliant white with dripping saliva. "You!" she spat, "You, who stole my destiny...

who stole my life...that made me what I am today!" Just as suddenly as she had grabbed my throat she released and spun away from me, as she did so she screamed out an agonising growl that was so shrill that I instinctively placed my hands over my ears to block out the sound.

I think it was probably at this moment that I realised that Rose was insane. Although the thought had crossed my mind several times in the few minutes prior to her outburst, there was a tone to her ranting voice that somehow finally confirmed the fact. Something had happened to her when she had become a vampire, I was not sure what, but I knew that for some reason her mind had been unable to cope with the change. I had heard Robert, in the past, mention that some people lose their sanity in the process of changing. However, I had never witnessed this strange phenomenon before, and in all truth I would not wish to witness it again. For most vampires are dangerous, but an insane vampire is not only totally unpredictable, but a danger to all.

When she had calmed down, and had once again turned her crazed eyes in my direction, I said, "Will you fetch Robert?"

"Yes, but I will not return. For I know that I shall rip out your heart and pierce it with the sharpest stake I can find, if I were to do so...and not even Robert will be able to stop me!"

"So be it..." I whispered with my head angled towards the floor. I remained this way until I heard her depart and then I lifted my weeping face and I screamed and screamed. I was so angry at the beast she had become and at the fact that changing into a vampire had caused this disgusting metamorphosis in one that was so gentle. I then sobbed in despair for the wrong I had done and then for the realisation that it was my task to reverse it—and how on earth was I going to accomplish that feat?

Chapter Eighteen

I heard Robert's soft tread, and smelt his rich musky smell, an aroma that was unique and his alone, before I saw him. I then heard his deep musical voice utter my name, the sound of which was like the yearning of the saddest song, and I turned to look into the eyes that had haunted me for a century.

"Robert..." I whispered. My voice, even to my own ears, sounded heartbroken and wistful.

"Gwen..." he replied, his voice soft like my own. His gaze drank in my face as if searching for something he had misplaced, and as a solitary tear fell from my lashes, his face changed and he smiled, and it was obvious from that smile, that he had found what he was looking for.

My gaze lingered on his perfect features, and I watched him in wonder. How could one ever forget the perfection that was his alone? The all-male vibrancy, sensuality, and pure sexual magnetism that had collided in pure exquisiteness to make the being that stood in front of me.

I placed one foot in front of the other as if in a dream, and suddenly I was in his embrace, and our lips tangled in a frenzy of love and lust. I drank from him.

Once again, I tasted the blood that flowed through his veins—blood that tasted like the purest wine—aged and rich. I felt his fangs pierce my neck, lips, and breasts, and I screamed from pure ecstasy as he tasted the love that flowed through my body.

Over, and over again, we shared our love, blood, and bodies with each other. How beautiful was the love we shared, for I realised that I had never loved anyone as I loved Robert, and I knew from that moment on, that I would never love another. And so, I surrendered my soul to him and as we blended our bodies and I cried out his name, I committed every part of him to memory. Thus I knew that I would always remember what it felt like to be truly loved and in love, now, and for all time.

The hours we spent together were magical. How could I have forgotten the love and tenderness we had shared in the past, but then, maybe our love had not been as strong before. Maybe, it was the bittersweet rekindling of lost love that made our joining so marvellous and awe-inspiring. However, no matter what the reason, I realised that he was and would always be the love of my life, and it didn't matter if I hated the fact—there was no way of changing it.

Chapter Nineteen

I awoke sometime later to find myself engulfed in Robert's arms with our bodies still joined and our hearts beating as one. As much as I loved the feeling of Robert inside of me, my leg was trapped underneath him, and felt numb and uncomfortable, and so I gently tried to prise it out without waking him.

"Where do you think you're going?" he muttered sleepily.

"I need to move," I whispered in return.

"No! I do not want you to move...I need to talk to you about something..."

My heart sank as he spoke. I knew, without confirmation, what he wanted to talk about, and I was not keen on pursuing the conversation.

"Must we talk of the past?" I said, hoping to delay the words I had no wish to hear. However, my tactic failed to work and Robert continued, "It is not the past that concerns me, Gwen, but the future, and in particular, Rose."

"I know what you are going to say!" I said, my words leaving my mouth in a rush. "I know...and I cannot do what you will ask me to do...please, oh please do not ask me..."

"Gwen..." He spoke my name softly, "I...we...we have no other choice...I wish with all my heart that we did...but she must be stopped."

"But why me?" I asked him, although in truth I already knew the answer.

"Because I told you that she was too weak, when she was just a small babe in arms. I sensed then, that she would mentally be too weak to be able to live our way of our life, and so I thought of a way that would give her life a purpose, and so rather than simply kill her—she was to be a sacrifice. However you, Gwen, made that impossible, and instead you sacrificed Matilda's life to enable you to steal Rose and ensure she lived."

He had risen up from the floor in the middle of his speech and had started to pace the room, and as he spoke about Matilda, he turned and looked at me with pain etched into his handsome face. After a long pause, which seemed to etch his pain into every stone in the chateau, and change the atmosphere completely, he continued, "I hated you, Gwen...and at first, I wanted to eradicate you from the face of the earth...but I soon realised that you had created your own punishment, for one day in the future, you would have need to face the ultimate pain!"

"I cannot...surely you can see that!" I mumbled, my voice, like an animal in the last throes of death, yearning, and hopelessly pleading for life.

"But you must! Do you know how many young lives she has taken...not for hunger, or need, but for sport! I have witnessed her, surrounded by countless young bodies—babies of not more than two years in age, and not one of them slaughtered for their blood. Nay...she had taken not one sip, and when I asked her why? She laughed and she said she liked the thrill of the kill! Whole families gone...eradicated by an insane mind!"

"Oh, you mean like you eradicated Tom's family!" I shouted at him as I jumped to my feet—anger simmering in the pit of my gut at the extent of his hypocrisy.

"I had my reasons for their deaths," he said, his voice low.

"Oh no...no you did not...you killed them before you had seen me...before you knew that I carried Henry inside of me."

"No, Gwen. I was there on the night that you conceived my son...high above you, in the branches of the huge oak in the sweet meadow. I watched you thrash and scream under your young lover, and I knew that I wanted the child you conceived on that cold and frosty night...and so I waited...and when the time was right...I came for you."

I sat down heavily on the bench that resided under the window in the salon—totally shocked and bewildered by his words.

"You were there?" I asked, my voice a whisper.

"Yes...I witnessed you seduce your lover, and although it was a freezing night, and he had no wish to bed you...you bewitched him with your seductiveness and your strength of will. You were so strong...so much stronger than your lover, not in body of course, but in mind...and I knew that you would produce a great man—a man of strength!"

"So I am to blame for their deaths?" I said, more to myself than to Robert.

"No, you were not! You were simply you! Their deaths were just part of their destinies and your life, thus far, is part of your own destiny...but now we must look to the future."

"And what is the future?" I asked him. I knew what he was going to say, but I needed him to say the words aloud.

"You must kill Rose and stop her evil, and in doing so undo the wrongs you have done."

"And if I am unable to kill her?" I asked him, my voice quivering with fear.

"Then I will have no other choice than that of letting her loose on the children of France, and I will also kill your maid who waits for you, shaking in the barn...

for you must be punished, Gwen. However, if you do as I ask, then I shall let you leave...and I will remind you, that by killing Rose you are saving many children—I am sure, my sweet, that your delightful compassion will guide you in the choice that you make."

I did not answer him. I could not! I waited patiently for him to walk from the salon, and then I placed my head in my hands and wept, for I already knew what choice I would make—and I hated myself for it.

Chapter Twenty

Robert returned a few hours later to find me prone on the floor. Sobs were still vibrating loudly from my body, and when he asked me if I had made my decision, it took me a few moments to answer.

"I do not have a choice in the matter," I stated when I was finally able to speak. "I cannot continue to allow her to take so many young lives...it is immoral even by our standards, but it is so difficult...how can I...how can I kill the child of my heart?"

"Because you must, Gwen! She cannot be allowed to live! She is a danger to herself and all surrounding her. I know you will never believe me, but I wish her fate had turned out differently. I had hoped that for once I was wrong, and her destiny was different. However, I am not God, and I cannot change her fate, and so she must die...for we will all suffer if she does not."

I knew he spoke the truth, and that it was not only his intention to punish me. However, knowing something was right and needed doing, was completely different than actually doing the deed. I hung my head for a moment, completely lost in the misery I must face, when suddenly something he said struck me, and rising my head I voiced my thoughts.

"You said you are not God, do you actually believe in God?"

"Do you doubt that God exists, Gwen?" he asked me, but continued before I could reply to his question. "How can there not be God, after all we were all created...yes...even we were created! For you see, Gwen, if there is good then there must be evil in order to challenge and test the good. We were created for this reason, and we are a punishment for man's betrayal of good...if man can conquer us...then he will conquer his own capacity to destroy all that he holds dear to him..."

"But, how...how do you know all of this?" I asked him, my bewilderment causing my voice to quiver.

"It does not matter how I know...I have already said too much..." he said as he turned away from me.

"Please tell me, Robert," I begged, "If something should happen to you...then the truth of our creation will be lost."

"No! It will never be lost! I, unlike you, can never be killed...I was the first vampire...and I shall be the last!"

"I do not understand...how is that possible? How old are you?"

"Enough!" he shouted as he turned back towards me. "I have said all that I am willing to say...now you must answer my question. Will you undo the wrongs you have done?"

"Yes...for I have no choice in the matter, but you must give me a few days...I need time to prepare myself for that which will break my heart," I said, a sob once again breaking my voice.

"Very well. However, I will send Rose to you in three days," he said, and then reaching into the folds of his cloak he withdrew a dagger made of wood and handed it to me. "This dagger will enable you to get close to Rose without alerting her of your intentions." I took the dagger from him and held it flat in my hand, with the other hand I touched the wooden blade and was shocked to feel how sharp it was.

"Why it is almost as sharp as a metal blade...how is that possible?" I said, once more weighing the black wood in my hand.

"It was given to me a very long time ago...I know not how it was made..." he muttered. I did not believe him, but I refrained from asking him more questions.

"When you have thrust the dagger into Rose's heart, leave it embedded, and I will remove it when I return to the chateau. I will then give you until sundown to vacate the chateau...because although I believe the task I have set you is punishment enough for that of taking Matilda's life...I am afraid that your son does not agree with me...he will have no qualms about killing you."

I gasped at his words, for I was hoping that it would be possible for me to once again meet my son, and then his son, and my great-great-grandchild.

"So he still hates me?" I foolishly asked, already knowing the answer.

"Yes, it is so...and it is for the best if you know that you will not change his mind, Gwen...he is set against you and there is nothing you or I can do to change his opinion."

I digested his words and I realised that Robert was yet again offering me good advice, and that I would do well, this time, to take heed of it.

"So be it..." I said sadly, "But, what about us?"

"There can be no us, Gwen...my place is to be beside Henry...and you...well, I am sure that you will find your own way."

"But will we ever meet again?" I asked, tears once more brimming in my eyes.

"I do not doubt that we shall...and I believe we will once again become lovers, but also enemies, for I believe that you are my nemesis, Gwen. You challenge me like no other!"

I smiled at his words and I, like him, did not doubt that they were true.

I then stood on my tiptoes and gently placed my lips to his, and closing my eyes I, just for a few moments, inhaled his intoxicating being. I did not drink of his blood, nor did he partake of mine. We instead shared a chaste and loving kiss, not as vampires, but as lovers, and when we pulled apart, he turned and walked away; the kiss was, for the moment at least, our goodbye.

Chapter Twenty-One

Oh, how tortuous were the days and nights that followed Robert's visit. I so wanted to run—run to the furthest corner of the earth where I could hide from the despair that ripped my soul apart. However, I knew that I would never escape Rose, or the extent of her madness. Her wild, insane, eyes would haunt me for all time, and finally, I would have no choice but to return and undo the wrong I had done.

I was alone in my misery. For I had sent Jeanne away to stay at an inn in Bordeaux, I was afraid for her safety, and bade her wait there until I joined her. And so in my despair, I sat for two days, not partaking of blood, but instead reading Rose's journal. I searched for her in the words, searched for the loving and beautiful girl that she had once been, but alas my searching was in vain.

The girl in the journal no longer existed, and so desperate was I to find her, that my finger started to trace the words of her quill in the hope, that just maybe, I would locate her soul if my skin was connected to the page.

However, it was a wasted exercise, and I realised that although I was able to connect to the girl who had bestowed all of her emotions on the pages of the journal, that girl lived a long time ago, and bore not one single resemblance to the vampire she had become.

I think it was this realisation that finally gave me the inner strength to prepare myself for the hellish task Robert had set me. And so on the third day I packed my clothes and coffers into a chest, and then I carefully placed Rose's journal on top. In the pages of the journal resided the real Rose—the child of my heart—but she had died almost half a century ago. The vampire I was to destroy was but a shell that resembled her in body only, and by placing Rose's journal in my chest, I had, in my own mind, buried the child that she had once been. Slowly, I dragged the chest out to the barn, and loaded it onto the cart that would carry me away from the chateau for the last time. I groomed and tacked up the carthorse, and tied him securely, and then did the same with my own horse, which would be secured to the back of the cart until I reached Jeanne in Bordeaux. Thus, having buried Rose, I returned to the salon, and having already stowed the dagger Robert had given me into the folds of my gown, I sat and I waited.

I know not how long it was before I detected the sweet and cloying smell that signalled that Rose had entered the chateau. However, the scent of her engulfed my senses, and bile arose in my throat, for I now knew that the stench that clung to her, was in fact, the breath and fragrance of all the young lives she had stolen. I did not move or stand, for I did not want to alert her to any changes in the way I felt about her, or rather, the girl she once was.

"Bonjour, Maman," she sneered as she passed through the doorway into the salon.
"Bonjour," I answered in a soft voice.
"I see that you failed to heed my warning," she said, her words again accompanied by the strange manic giggle from a few days earlier.
"I will not leave my home...if you must take my life...well then so be it!"
"Oh, Maman, how sweet and kind you are...and how um...let me think...ah yes, how ridiculous you are!"

Her eyes were now focused on me, I could feel them burning into my skin, and I knew that she wished me to look up and witness the evil behind her penetrating stare.

After a few moments I complied, and tried not to cringe at the beast I saw lurking in their depths.

"I sicken you, Maman...I can see it in your gaze..." I shrugged my shoulders, not trusting myself to speak.

"Oh dear...and so quiet...I thought you would have least put up some sort of a fight!" she hissed, her body bending over mine like a poised arrow ready to pierce its target.

"I have no wish to fight you, Rose..." I said softly as I stared into her twisted face, which was, to my utter relief, unrecognisable from the Rose I had once loved and cherished. As I stared up into her demonic face, my hand gripped the dagger hidden in the folds of my gown, and before she could utter another word I thrust it upwards into her chest. "I must kill you..." I whispered as tears filled my eyes.

I held her lifeless body in my arms for a moment, and then slowly, whilst holding her head to my chest, I lowered her body to the floor, and moving up slightly, gently cradled her beautiful face in my arms. I watched, in agony, as her eyes, the eyes that so resembled my own, flickered in disbelief, and then for the first time, in what I imagined was a very long time, her eyes softened and she smiled.

"Maman...Maman...you...you...love me still?" she gasped.

"Always..." I whispered as I held her tighter, my body rocking back and forth. A smile once more graced her sweet lips, and it was a smile that I had thought to never see again, for it was sweet and gentle—it was Rose.

"Thank you, Maman..."

"Do not speak, my sweet," I muttered, my voice catching from the sobs that vibrated through my body.

"But...but, I must...you released me, Maman...please do not cry...for I am..." Her voice failed for a moment and her face distorted with the pain. "I am free, Maman...I am forgiven...see...they have come for me..." Following her gaze, I instantly gasped, for the salon glowed with thousands of twinkling stars of light. Small glowing balls filled with searing, but beautiful colours, circled like butterflies above us.

"But how is it possible?" I whispered, my voice full of wonder, "We...we are evil..." Pulling my gaze from the mesmerising beauty that surrounded me, I looked into Rose's eyes and whispered, "How is it possible, Rose?"

Blood now flowed freely from the corners of her soft lips, and I felt panic rise through my body as I realised that she only had a few moments left.

"No...no...please stay," I begged, gathering her more tightly into my arms.

"It is time," she said, lifting her hand to my cheek, "You must search for the answers, my dearest Maman..." she whispered and closing her eyes, her last words echoed breathlessly around the salon walls. "I love you, Maman..."

I then watched, spellbound, as a small, but perfectly formed ball of light gathered in her chest and flew upwards to join the others floating above me. My words of, "I love you too..." echoed throughout the salon, and then suddenly stopped, and with the sound of my voice went the wondrous lights, and I was left holding Rose's lifeless, but peaceful body in my arms.

I waited for the lights to return, but of course they did not, and after a while I placed Rose's body on the floor and slowly stood up. I did not have long before Robert, Henry, and the others made their way to the chateau, and it was vital that I leave. I knew without doubt that I had witnessed the collecting of Rose's soul for a reason. However, I did not know that reason, not yet, but I intended to find out.

With what I believed was one last look at Rose, I started to walk towards the salon doorway and away from the chateau, but something stopped me, and I turned back towards her. I instantly noticed the dagger protruding from her chest, and I knew that I must take it with me, for instinct told me that it was somehow connected to my quest. I knelt down beside her body and withdrew the wood from her chest. However, I did not cry, for I knew that she was happy at last, and knowing this I would mourn her no more. I gently kissed her forehead, and then quickly made my way to the barn. Moments later I was on my way away from the chateau, not once did I look back, for it was with a sigh of relief that I rode away with the knowledge that I would never see its sinister walls ever again.

Part V

Chapter Twenty-Two

Gwen

1627

I reached the inn where Jeanne was staying just after sundown, and although I was emotionally tired, I did not dare stay in the comforting warmth by the beckoning fire. I was worried that Henry would be tempted to follow me, but more so that Robert would, by this time, know that I had stolen his dagger and want it back. Instead I paid the innkeeper, bade him farewell, and shortly after my arrival we were on our way.

I drove the cart through the night whilst Jeanne slept in the back, the sounds of the night, the clank of the wheels, and Jeanne's soft snores my only company. Not that I minded. I was still lost in the wondrous scene I had witnessed in the salon earlier that day. My mind constantly replayed the event, searching for a clue to focus on, and in doing so enable me to plan our destination. Nevertheless, no matter how I tried, I was unable to grasp an idea to cling to, and after a while I gave up.

For I realised that the events were too recent for me to unravel, and for once I must sit back and really think about what I intended to do.

Instead, I willed my mind to search through the events of the past few days. I recalled Robert's face, his tender words, and the exquisite moments that we had shared. I thought about what he had said about us being created by God, the dagger, and finally of Rose, and the release of her poor, but in the end, beautiful soul. I was sure all the events were connected, but I was confused by that connection. However, I had discovered a fact that was startling for me to comprehend. I was vital to unfolding the mystery and I had been chosen, by someone, or something, maybe even that to which Robert had referred to as 'God', to pursue the quest for truth-it was my destiny, and I think it was a destiny pre-ordained a long time before I had become a vampire, maybe even before I was born.

These thoughts left me excited, but also fearful, after all I had been, and in many ways still was, a simple farm girl. I was not in any way, shape, or form, a woman of consequence. I had no education or refined manners and apart from Jeanne, I was alone in the world, without an army or even a manservant. However, for some unknown reason I had been chosen, and I intended to try and find my way through the maze of unknowns and hopefully find the answers to my questions.

It was as the sun was breaking scarlet in the dark murky sky that I was roused from my jumbled thoughts. The smell of human death invaded my senses, and the sickening stench of old and rotten blood filled and invaded my mouth with its clinging odour. Pulling the horse to a standstill, I listened intently to the sounds around me.

A muffling sound, similar to that of a young piglet suckling on a sow, drifted on the wind. Tying the horse and cart to a jutting branch, I jumped down and made my way carefully through the overgrown forest. I had walked for maybe a mile when I noticed a small and unkempt stone dwelling nestling in the valley below me.

Realising that it was from the dwelling that the evil stench and muffling sounds were coming, I made my way swiftly down the incline towards the cottage.

I investigated the barn first; it housed some pigs, a cow, and several chickens, albeit they were all starving and looked near to death. However, the stench or the muffling sounds did not come from the barn, and so I moved with stealth towards the cottage. It seemed, as I entered that small dark space, that I had stepped back in time, for lying prone across the table, her throat ripped out, was an old maid. Her dead and lifeless eyes stared towards the ceiling, and her toothless mouth stretched wide in a soundless scream.

So shocked was I by the sight that I stumbled backwards and toppled over a flat stone that had been used to hold the door open. Quickly I scurried to my feet, embarrassed to be so nervous of death, and once more made my way through the doorway. I glanced at the dead woman fleetingly, but refused to be intimidated by the sight of her, even if she did remind me of the way I had found poor Martha all those years ago.

Just as I did all those years ago, I made my way up the rickety ladder that climbed to the floor above, and slowly picked my way through the slaughtered bodies scattered about the floor.

The stench was overpowering, and I wanted nothing more than to run from the room and never return. However, it was from this room that I had heard the muffling sounds, and to me it signalled that life resided somewhere in the dark recesses.

I stood still as I surveyed the room. As far as I could tell there were five dead bodies, consisting of one adult male, a youngish woman, and three small children. I was certain that the family had been slaughtered by a vampire, and a very cruel and merciless one at that. Instantly, I thought of Rose, and again I felt relieved that I had released her from the madness that had consumed her and her victims.

I waited patiently for the survivor to show him or herself, for I had no doubt that there was someone hiding in the room. However, due to the sickening smells surrounding me, I was unable to identify where they were hiding—and so I waited.

As anticipated, it did not take long before fear overtook the stowaway, and like a flash, a young boy, no more than four years of age, made a dash for the opening that led below.

I quickly caught him, and holding him under my arm made my way down the ladder, through the doorway, and out into the early morning sunshine. I then looked at the child, and instantly my heart filled with compassion and love, for he was so very afraid, and yet still he fought me gallantly. When his strength had gone, and he could only make soft mewing sounds—he looked up into my face. His eyes were huge, and shone like chips of black rock, glinting in his small wasted face, his mouth was cracked and sore from lack of food and water, and I could feel his small heart beating haphazardly, almost, but not quite ready to give into death.

Fear gleamed in his eyes as I bit into my wrist, and his small fist flew out in an attempt to stop me, but he was too close to death to defend, what I am sure, he thought were his last moments of life. I positioned him so I was able to hold him securely, and I held my wrist to his lips, I then gently prised his mouth open and fed him my blood.

It was not long before his breathing, heartbeat, and the colour in his face had returned to normal. However, he had drifted into a deep sleep and so I placed his small weak body on a patch of lush grass, and after checking that he was resting peacefully and would sleep for a while, I started to walk back through the forest.

Chapter Twenty-Three

Jeanne and I returned to the cottage to find the boy still asleep where I had placed him. I was relieved that he had not awoken and strayed whilst I was away, and by the look of her face, so was Jeanne.

While he slept we quickly buried the dead, cleaned, and fed the animals. For we were both concerned for how he would be affected if he awoke to find the bodies of his loved ones still scattered about the farm. Although, we had worked quickly, expecting him to wake at any time, we had no need to, for he did not wake until two days after I had fed him my blood.

When he did awake, he was very afraid, and his eyes once more shone with unshed tears. However, he soon became accustomed to us, or perhaps I should say Jeanne. He was still afraid of me, and would cower slightly when I entered the room, but of course that was to be expected, after all he knew that I was similar in nature to the beast that slaughtered his family. I did not hold my wrist to his lips again, but instead let my blood flow into a glass of milk, thus ensuring that he got well.

I knew that he would be afraid if he knew he drank my blood, and so decided that this was the most palatable way for him consume that which I knew would make him well.

It was not long before he started to look healthy and he was out of the sickbed, following Jeanne around the farm. He had taken to her and she became, for him, his surrogate mother. I think for Jeanne this was also the case, for apart from the love she bestowed on me, I had never seen her so close to another person.

Nevertheless, the attack on his family had, we believed, unbalanced him and no matter how we both tried, we could not get him to speak. Jeanne suggested that maybe he had been born mute, but I didn't think so, after all I had heard him making the soft mewing sounds on the day I had found him. However, we were unable to get him to utter any words, and so we called him Charles, simply because when we read out a list of names, hoping to find one that sounded familiar to him—he smiled.

We stayed at the farm for several weeks. Jeanne was content to work the farm with Charles beside her, and I found the setting peaceful, which gave me time to think. I would sit every day, on the banks of the small stream that flowed through the farm, and think about Rose, the dagger, Robert, and about how everything was connected. I did not find the answers, but I did find some words engraved into the wood of the dagger. However, they were of a language that I was unfamiliar with, and so the discovery did not help me on my quest.

That was until one day a scene from the past replayed a memory that I had stowed away a long time ago. I had taken to searching through the events of my long life in a desperate attempt to find a clue that would help me find the direction I needed to take. So, as I once more replayed the past inside my mind, I stumbled on the memory of Robert holding Matilda's body in his arms, his anguished voice shouting out words in a language I was unable to understand. Instantly, I wondered if the words were of the same language as that which was engraved into the handle of the dagger.

It seemed likely that this could be the case, and I probed my memory over and over, searching for words that might resemble those engraved on the knife. However, the letters were strange, and I didn't know the sounds they made, when voiced alone or combined, and so had little hope of translating them.

I was unsure of the academic world. I had been born a poor and lowly farm girl, and didn't even know how to write my name until I had employed Pierre to coach Rose and had secretly engaged him to teach me. And although I had found joy in knowledge, I was by no means a scholar. However, I was not sure that even a tutor such as Pierre would be able to decipher the words. Suddenly an idea struck me, and jumping up from the bank, I decided that it was time for me to journey from the farm and to seek out someone with knowledge of languages—instinctively I knew that that person would be of a vocation that would normally be abhorrent to me—that person would be a priest.

Jumping up onto my horse, Juan, I called out to Jeanne that I was going in search of the nearest town. I had not ventured from the farm since we had found Charles, and I was unsure about where in the country we were actually now located.

However, I knew that the time had come to rectify this fact. I had spent long enough contemplating the course of action I should take, and now that Charles was recovered, and we had all settled down from the recent events, it was time to push on and find answers to the questions we had been set.

Chapter Twenty-Four

I followed an easterly direction when I left the farm, and after travelling about half a day I came upon the town of Agen. Agen, at this time, was no more than a town scattered around the Cathédrale Saint-Caprais d'Agen. I was surprised, albeit pleasantly, for I had not realised that we had travelled so far from Bordeaux. After making enquiries about the best local scholar, I was pointed in the direction of the cathedral, and so after leaving Juan at the local inn I headed towards the impressive building.

The air surrounding the walls of the Cathédrale Saint-Caprais d'Agen was calm and peaceful. However, the building up close was ravaged and unkempt, a result, I was later to discover, of the war of religion which took place in 1561. I entered the building and at first I was astounded by the regal beauty of the interior, and then surprised by the chill of the old stones, but even more so by the sight of chickens clucking and scratching about on the stone floor.

"Bonjour, madame, can I help you?"

I jumped at the sound of the echoing voice, for I had been so intent on studying the beauty of the building that I had not heard the soft tread of the monk who now stood before me.

"Oui, monsieur...I am told that I may be able to find a scholar within the walls of the Cathédrale Saint-Caprais d'Agen. I am in need of someone who specialises in languages."

The monk, who was middle-aged, was of a grimy appearance, and his eyes were like slits in his bloated toad-like face. He looked sly, and gave the impression of being slimy like the aforementioned toad. Instantly I knew that he was not a man to be trusted.

"Let me see what you have, I may be able to help you," he said as he extended his hand to me.

"Non...I wish to speak to a scholar...maybe a priest?" I answered, slowly backing away from him. His eyes narrowed further, and a flicker of irritation radiated from his greasy face. I knew that if I had met him a few weeks prior, I would have been delighted to rid the world of one that was so distasteful to me. Alas, I had changed, and although I fought the urge to sink my teeth deep into his throat—it was something that I still yearned to do.

"Mon Père, is busy...but I will ask him...wait here if you please," he said bowing his head, but his actions did not seem to be those of a monk, in fact they implied sarcasm rather than servitude and meekness. And I suddenly realised that he was a man who sought advancement and his ambition may be not only his own undoing, but probably that of all who came into contact with him.

I sat down on a roughly made, but adequate bench, and once more surveyed my surroundings. This was the first time I had entered a place of worship since I had become a vampire and I had forgotten the feelings of peace that a place such as this evoked in me. I smiled at the irony of how strange it was, that I, a vampire, and the epitome of evil, was resting in a place of worship with feelings of peace and faith flowing through my diseased being.

"Ahem...you wish to see me, mademoiselle?" I turned, somewhat startled by the voice behind me, and looked into an old, but gentle face. The priest was ancient, and lines crisscrossed his face, giving the impression of scars. His back was bent, and his hair was wispy and balding, but his eyes were those of a gentle being and shone from his face warmly, reminding me of the eyes of a doe or a gentle horse—they were beautiful.

"Oui, Mon Père...is it possible to speak with you in private?" I said, my eyes swivelling to the monk whom was standing behind the priest, his sly eyes missing nothing.

"Oui...of course...we will walk," he answered and then looking behind him towards the monk said, "André, you will stay and shoo the chickens outside..." Anger shone from the monk André's eyes, but he hid it well, and said in his irritating nasal voice, "As you wish, Mon Père..."

We walked in silence until we were out of earshot, and then the priest slowed and turning towards me, placed his old hand on my arm.

"I am sorry about André, he means well, but I am afraid he is a little...um...how do you say...nosey?"

"Oui..." I said smiling, although I was sure that André was a little bit more than nosey and in fact, was sly and manipulative. However, it was obvious that the priest tried to look for the good in people, and so I refrained from trying to enlighten him about the conniving monk. For it is said that ignorance is bliss and for the priest at least—I believed this to be so.

"Why do you need my help...my child?" he asked, his hand still resting on mine.

"I found this...um this...this dagger..." I said as I pulled the knife out from the folds of my cloak and handed it to him. "There is writing, but I do not know what language it is written in...I thought that maybe you would know?"

His old hands shook as he took the dagger, and I noticed that he had taken a sharp intake of breath as I spoke. Suddenly an expression of wonder radiated from his wrinkled face and he whispered, "It is glorious...glorious!" He didn't speak for a while after his first startled response, but his fingers traced the writing on the dagger and his breathing was rapid and shallow.

"Can I ask where you found this?" he finally asked, his eyes, now gleaming with excitement, arose to meet my own.
"I...um...I cannot lie to you, Mon Père, but I cannot tell you either...all I can say is that it is vital I trace its origins and that it is a matter of great importance," I said, my eyes not leaving his.
"I understand...but this is a rare find...it is old, maybe as old as Christ...and I believe it is not of this world...it is formed so perfectly...I am not sure that a man would be able to make this..." His voice was low, but I could hear the amazement behind his words.

"And the language?" I asked him, my voice also low and hushed.

"I cannot say for sure...but I believe you will need to travel to the east...and probably Rome...you may find answers...but be careful, child...many will want this..."

"I am able to take care of myself, Mon Père."

"Yes I know," he said, and then after taking a deep breath, continued, "I know what you are...but you are different than the others I have encountered...good remains in you, although you were born out of evil."

I hung my head, because I was ashamed that this man of God should know what I was and what I did to survive. Placing one of his twisted fingers under my chin, he lifted my head and said, "It is the compassion that remains inside of you that causes you to hang your head in shame...and it is this compassion that will conquer the evil you must face...be strong and you will succeed."

I smiled even though a solitary tear made its way down my cheek. "Thank you for your words, Mon Père," I said as I took the dagger from his outstretched hand and turned and walked away.

There was no need for more words, he had pointed me in the direction I must travel, and it was time to follow that path.

Chapter Twenty-Five

A terrible thirst for blood came upon me after I walked away from the cathedral, and although I hated the fact, especially after talking to the priest, that I must take from the innocent, I knew that I must drink, in order to survive and follow my destined path. However, I had decided that I would no longer take from and then leave my victims weak and defenceless. I had therefore concluded that after feeding from my chosen food, I would then trickle a small amount of my blood into their mouths, therefore ensuring their continued survival.

It did not take me long to find what I was looking for. A much used and abused whore had passed out from the consumption of excessive amounts of wine, and lay prone and alone, along the filthy dark alley that ran behind the inn where I had left my horse, Juan. Her blood tasted foul, and was thick and syrupy, which indicated to me that although she was alive for the moment, it would not be very many weeks before her addiction killed her. The fact that I would extend her life by a considerable amount by feeding her my blood—made taking from her so much easier.

It is strange how the taste of blood differs from person to person. In the young it is sweet and untainted by life, sometimes in the aged it can be warm and spiced, but if the donor has lived a squalid lifestyle, then the blood can sometimes be unpalatable. Thus, so it was with the whore and although her blood nourished and fed my hunger—the taste left much to be desired.

I had just finished drinking from her liberally, and replenishing her blood with my own, when I heard a noise behind me. After quickly wiping my mouth, I jumped up and turned to see who had spied on me in my moment of depravity. The monk from the cathedral lounged against the grimy wall, and it was obvious from his sly grin that he had been watching me for quite some time.

"What do you want?" I asked, my voice gruff and full of disdain.
"To become as you are," he answered simply, his eyes glinting with desperate need.
"And what is that?" I asked him, trying desperately to buy the time to allow me to decide what to do with him. However, one thing was for certain—I did not want to commit murder.

"I am sure I have no need to tell you what you are...or how the people of the town will react when they are told about the beast they have in their midst. Mon Père will not be able to save you, nor I, that is if I was so inclined. It is your choice, mademoiselle."

Anger stampeded like a raging ball through my body. I flew towards André, smashing his ugly bloated body against the wall—my hand gripped his sweating neck and ached to twist and end his worthless life.

"I can kill you before you have the time to think about it, you disgusting weasel..." I growled at him. My fangs had grown, and I could tell from the fear written upon his face that my eyes glowed with opaque menace, promising destruction and death.

"Do you think that I would turn one such as you?" I whispered in a deep growl, "A sly two-faced toad, set free to murder and pillage innocence...I would rather die first!" I stared straight into his eyes, which were for the first time, not sly and heavily hooded, but wide and staring with fear.

"You will never speak of this day...do you hear me?" I whispered and then waited for his answer.

"Oui, mademoiselle..." His pupils grew larger, a sign that he was under my spell and he had succumbed to being bewitched.

"You will never speak about me...do you understand?" Once again he voiced his compliance.

When I was sure that he was would forget about my existence—I dropped him to the floor. I was still battling the urge to kill him, but instead kicked him, and felt the rage inside me evaporate as I heard his groan of pain. Although it was just a small victory, hearing his cry gave me the feeling of triumph I craved. After all, I was still a vampire and I still needed to witness a little pain, in order to quell the instinctive killer that lurked deep down inside.

However, I was still concerned. Bewitching didn't always work, and if it did, the effects did not always last. Although it was a rare occurrence, some people were able to battle against it and regain their memory. I do not know why, but I had an overwhelming feeling that André would be one of the few who would manage to do this, and the thought left me very nervous.

Earlier that day, after talking to the priest, I had decided that it was best if I left Jeanne and Charles at the farm whilst I made my journey to Rome.

However, the incident with André suddenly changed my mind, and as I rode away from the town I decided that we would all be making the journey to Rome. For I believed I had made an enemy, and I knew from past experience that enemies took out their wrath on the ones I loved.

Chapter Twenty-Six

On my return to the farm I made haste in arranging our departure. Jeanne was not happy, but as in all things, she bowed to my wishes. Charles surprised me by being excited by the forthcoming adventure, but I guessed that the farm held too many bad memories for him, and although he still refused to speak, a smile would grace his lips as I talked of the journey we were to undertake. When I spoke of Rome and the exotic lands of the east, he would suddenly climb onto my lap and stare into my face. I think that we were both shocked the first time he did this, for up until that time he had never approached me. I smiled down into his enchanting face, and continued to speak of the distant lands. I even found myself making up facts in the hope that his small warm body would stay snuggled to mine. Alas, this was not always the case, and after a while he would grow bored and jump down to chase the chickens or throw a stone.

Two days after my return from Agen, we started eastward on our journey to Rome. I had instructed Jeanne to free the animals in the barn, much to her disapproval, for she had intended to sell them at market.

However, the closest town was Agen, and I was adamant that we must bypass the small but bustling streets. André was still in the forefront of my mind, and I didn't want to risk him seeing me and the event jogging his memory. So I was insistent that we avoid the town.

And so we started our journey into the unknown—a child, an old woman, and a vampire. What a strange group of adventurers we made, but nonetheless, I would wish for no others to accompany me. That our journey would be dangerous, I had no doubt. For we would be entering a cavern filled with the unknown, or should I say the hidden, and secrets have a tendency to be hidden by those who do not want them found. Thus, it was likely that we could be killed, and that our quest would always be left undiscovered, but that was a chance I was willing to take.

Once more my life was to take a new direction, but this time I embraced the change. For I felt that at long last my life had meaning, and that meaning was to enable me to discover the true story of vampirism.

I was sure that my quest was to unravel a mystery. A mystery that told the story of our creation and one that had remained a secret for thousands of years. I had no doubt what I would do with this knowledge—I would kill Robert, and find the means to extinguish my life, and the life of all other vampires.

To be continued...

Coming soon…

Echoes of Kin, (book two in the Mary Howard Supernatural Mysteries Series). Nov 2014

Secrets in the Sand, (book four in the Vampire series). Feb 2015

Sins Forgotten, (book five in the Vampire series). May 2015

The Betrayers Kiss, (book six in the Vampire series). Aug 2015

Book three in the, *Mary Howard Supernatural Mysteries Series*. Dec 2015

<<<<>>>>

Excerpt from Death Whispers

(Mary Howard Supernatural Mysteries Series)

Chapter One

Her feet tingled from the cold, in fact, every part of her ached with a damp chill. The day had started well enough with only a touch of ground frost, which normally was a good sign, and usually a cold but sunny day was bound to follow. However, today seemed to be the exception, and it had rained and rained.

Mary had set out on her two mile walk into the pretty market town of Petersfield, when the sun was shining and the air was crisp. It was therefore a little bit irritating, actually very irritating when, after buying her groceries, popping into the bank, and having a well earned latte at Costa's, she had started to make her two mile trek home, only to experience the heavens suddenly opening and soaking her to the skin.

When she finally reached her tumbledown (falling down might be more apt) cottage, which was nestled on the outskirts of a very pretty, very tiny village; which was bizarrely named Sheet, she was tired, cold, aching, and felt very, very, irritated.

Peeling off her very thick, absolutely sodden, woollen cardigan, which she had worn instead of a mac; believing it would protect her from the cold, she made her way to her bedroom. Of course, the wet cardigan, wet cords, wet shoes, in fact wet everything had only served to weigh her down heavily, and she smelled like a hairy wet dog, and presumed that she looked like one too.

Peering into the mirror which sat on top of her dressing table, she no longer presumed, but knew, she looked like the aforementioned hairy wet dog. Scurrying out of her clothes, she quickly changed into her fluffy pj's and warm bed socks, and then proceeded to jump head first into her duvet and snuggle down into the warmth. "*Ah bliss,*" she mumbled in quiet satisfaction, she then closed her eyes and deliberated on what she was going to do for the rest of the day.

Mary was a writer; well, she liked to think she was. Although, if her book sales were anything to go by, she wasn't really succeeding at her chosen profession. She pretended that it didn't matter to her very much, but the truth was that it did matter; very much, if she was being brutally honest.

Closing her eyes tightly she tried to visualise her grandmother. Her inspiration, the warmth in her life, and the very essence of her being, because for Mary, her grandmother was the place she called home. However, much to her irritation, she found it difficult to connect to the visualisation, and with a sigh and "*blast it,*" hissing from her lips, Mary threw back the duvet and marched into the kitchen to make herself a cup of tea.

Figures...just bloody figures, she thought as she looked out of the kitchen window at the now perfect sunny January morning. Turning from the window and clenching her cold hands around her warm mug of tea, she made her way into the study.

The study was her favourite room in the cottage, it was snug and warm, or would be when the open fire started crackling in the grate. With this in mind; she took the box of matches from the mantle, struck a match, and carefully placed the small flame into the paper and kindling that she had prepared before her shopping expedition to Petersfield.
She waited until the kindling was roaring and then emptied a small bucket of coal and a couple of dry logs on top of the flames.

She watched for a moment, and after satisfying herself that the coal and logs would take hold, she made her way over to an old leather chair that stood in front of a huge antique walnut desk, and sunk in to its welcoming folds.

She had walked into the study with the intention of continuing where she had left off with her current story. However, she found that she was unable to open her laptop, not because it wouldn't open, but because she didn't want to. *What's the bloody point,* she thought, *it's no better than anything I've written in the past, it'll flop, just like they all flop.*

Laying her head back against the old, tattered, but soft and familiar leather of the chair, Mary tried to figure out where she was going wrong. She knew that most people would look at her life and think she had it made, and she wasn't so stupid or selfish not to know that they were probably right.

She was twenty-two, owned her cottage outright (even if it was falling down). She also had more money in the bank then it was likely she would ever, in her lifetime, be able to spend.

However, she had no one to share her wealth with. Her parents had died in a car crash when she was just two years old, and her grandmother, whom she had lived with ever since her parents died, had died just under a year previously.

It was her grandmother whom she missed the most. She found it difficult to remember her parents, but her grandmother had always been there for her. She missed her presence, her beauty and kindness, and the way they would discuss their writing; warm by the fire, with her grandmother giving, but also receiving Mary's constructive criticism. After all her grandmother was one of England's greatest authors. Victoria Howard was known throughout the world for her horrific and hugely popular, 'Nightfall Mysteries'. When the great Victoria Howard died, she bequeathed the whole of her vast fortune to her granddaughter, but with Victoria went the extent of her family - Mary was the sole remaining member, she was to all intents and purposes, alone.

Well, apart from one person, her best friend Kate, but Kate lived in London, and she mixed with the famous and wealthy jet-setting types.

It was the type of life that didn't really suit Mary, who was shy and reserved, and a woman who blushed at the mere mention of a dirty joke.

They did, however, spend part of the year together, normally when Kate felt she needed the peace and tranquility that only the leafy country lanes of Hampshire could offer her. She would arrive like a whirlwind, taking over Mary's life, and just as suddenly vanish back to her world of glitz and glamour. Thus leaving Mary to feel even lonelier then she had before Kate had arrived. Mary didn't really mind. It had been the same when they were children, so why should it be any different now?

Kate was the daughter of the late, but very well remembered, Edward Windell, Victoria Howard's long time agent and lover. Edwards's wife had died giving birth to Kate, and so it was that Mary's grandmother eventually become his lover. It seemed the whole world knew of the affair, but no one talked of it. Least of all the two children that happily played together in their own little world, whilst their guardians discussed business, and, as both the children later realised, partook of pleasure.

Nowadays Kate would laugh about the relationship, often saying that she wished Victoria and Edward had married, that way she and Mary would have indeed been sisters. Mary would retort that she felt like they were sisters anyway so it didn't really make any difference.

However, she had never understood their relationship. She had tried; but to her, love was about flowers, hearts, and kisses. Not about a quick bunk up in the back toilet (she had actually walked in on the lovers in the said toilet one day). She believed in love, and that was why she chose to write about love. However, as Kate had so often pointed out to her, "To be able to write about a subject, Mary, you need to understand it." She knew this and if anyone had asked, she would have been ashamed to admit that she was twenty-two years old and had never been kissed; actually she had never even come close to being kissed. She knew that was why readers of her books had criticised the love scenes, and why some had stated that her books reminded them of fairy tales. She needed to understand all of the emotions she wrote about, and not guess at them. But how was she able to do that, when to even smile at someone of the opposite sex resulted in a bright red blush brightly colouring her skin?

Mary pushed herself up from the leather chair; walked to the fireside, threw on a couple of logs, and then ambled over to the window. She saw a shadow out of the corner of her eye, but ignored it. Instead, her thoughts lingered on her love life, or lack of. When the shadow moved closer, she turned and shouted angrily at the air,

"And how am I meant to meet a man when I have you lot trailing behind me the whole bloody time?"

Grabbing her cup, she slammed out of the study, and made her way towards the kitchen. The shadow didn't follow.

Mary inhaled deep breaths in an attempt at calming herself down. By the time she had entered the kitchen she had succeeded, well almost. She looked up at the clock and winced; Dawn, her grandmother's daily cleaner would arrive soon, and although Mary didn't really need her services, she was loath to let her go. Dawn had worked for Victoria for thirty years, she was part of Mary's home, and she and the gardener Dan were the only company Mary had on a daily basis. They were part of her life in the cottage, always had been, and as far as she was concerned, always would be.

Mary knew that Dawn would moan if she found her dressed in pj's, and wearily walked back into her bedroom and got dressed in old jeans, and an over-sized warm jumper. Just as she had finished dressing she heard the back door slam, and she felt her spirits lighten at the thought of exchanging a few words with Dawn.

"Hello, my sweetheart," Dawn said as Mary walked into the kitchen, "You alright, my lovely?"

"Yes I'm okay. I got soaked in that downpour earlier, and got a bit irritated about it, but I'm fine now."

Dawn looked towards Mary, her eyes narrowing slightly.

"Why didn't you take the car, love?" she asked casually.

"I've decided to start walking...I need to shift some pounds, but I won't be doing that again in a hurry."

"Oh dear, Mary, you do get some strange ideas in your head, you do. You don't need to lose weight! Tell you what, I'll make us a cuppa before I get on...How does that sound?" Mary nodded in agreement, pulled out one of the chairs surrounding the table and flopped down onto it with a sigh.

After placing a cup of hot tea in front of Mary, Dawn placed her own on the table, pulled out a chair and said, "What's up, love, cos it looks like it's much more than just getting wet."

Mary didn't say anything for a moment. She then answered, her voice sad, "I feel like my life's going nowhere, my writing is crap, I have no friends, I've never had a relationship...and I have...well I have other problems."

Dawn frowned. *What other problems?* she thought. Instead she said, "You're the only one who can change all of that, love, you know that, don't you? Your gran would have told you that if she was here."

Mary nodded in agreement. *But she didn't know, nobody knew!* she silently shouted. Gulping down the last of her tea, Mary started to rise, but Dawn halted her progress by placing her hand on her arm.

"But it's more than that, isn't it, love?"

Can I tell her, will she think I'm crazy? Mary thought.

"You wouldn't believe me if I told you, Dawn," she said with a sigh.

"Well why don't ya try me and find out...it can't be that bad, love."

It is! She'll think I'm mad! she screamed to herself.

Her troubles rushed briefly through her mind, and she knew, just as Dawn had stated; that she was the only one who could change it all. Maybe, that change started with her admitting her problem.

"My sweet...?" Dawn asked, trying to shake Mary from the thoughts that had silenced her.

It's now or never, Mary thought and glanced up at Dawn's concerned face. She then dropped her head, and mumbled in a husky whisper, "*I see dead people!*"

Chapter Two

"Well I never! She always said you could...but you know what she was like, the woman believed in magic, for heaven's sake. She would've loved this, been her high delight it would have been..."

Mary watched, dumbfounded, as Dawn laughed.

"Did you *hear* what I said?" she asked, her voice high-pitched and squeaky.

"Yes, of course I did..." Dawn answered, a hint of laughter still vibrating in her voice.

"But I don't understand...What's...Well, what is *so funny*?" Mary snapped.

Dawn paused, realising Mary was far from happy at what she had just heard. She then clasped Mary's hand in her own and said, "Your gran, love, she knew you had the gift. She'd mention it to me often, telling me how you followed after her own mother. She said one day you would admit it, and until you did, you would never move on with your life...She was a clever woman, you know...not much passed her by, did it?"

They knew! All those years of thinking she was a lunatic, of thinking that people would think she was crazy, and all the time they knew!

Mary pushed back her chair and abruptly stood. She was angry, she was more than angry, she was fuming.

"*Well I'm glad you think it's funny, because I DON'T! All the years I thought I was mad, and it turns out...Oh my God! It turns out that you both knew...*" Mary paused in the middle of her rant. Her eyes were wide, and she was trembling and frantically hyperventilating.

"Now, love, don't be silly now. Your gran said you needed to admit it to yourself and..."

"*And what... She was wrong...I needed support,*" Mary said, and throwing her hands up in the air she started to move towards the door.

"Do you ever talk to her?"

Mary stood stock still in the doorway. Slowly, she turned towards Dawn, tears streaming down her face.

"No, no I don't...and that is what *so* annoying...The one person I want to talk to, and I can't! It stands to reason really, I'm a failure at everything, including talking to dead people!"

Dawn stumbled from her chair and pulled Mary into her arms. "Don't say that...don't ever say that, you're not a failure, you're wonderful...oh my poor, poor, girl."

Mary clung onto Dawn's warm, plump body, her tears running freely, soaking the older woman's shoulder.

"There, there...stop the tears now...come on, stop it...you'll be making yourself ill, you will."

Dawn pulled her towards the table and after pushing her back into a chair, grabbed some paper kitchen roll and put the kettle back on. Handing the kitchen roll, which served as a make-do hankie, to Mary, she said, "So why now, love...why tell me now? I mean after all these years, there must be a reason?"

Mary blew her nose and wiped her eyes. *Why now?* She repeated the question silently to herself.

She thought she knew why, but even so, it didn't make sense to her. How many times had she been visited by lost souls? Souls crying out for help, help that she didn't know how to give, and wasn't sure even if she did know, if she would. She hated her visitors, and whenever possible she had always tried to ignore their presence. She had always hoped that if she ignored them long enough they would, in the end, get the message and finally leave her alone. Nevertheless, her strategy had never worked, and the spirits still glided into her life without as much as an invitation or a by your leave.

Memories of childhood engulfed her. Visions of a small child, her head buried deep in a hot quilt, and her mouth urgently whispering the Lord's Prayer in an attempt to stave off the dreaded spirits. So very afraid to glimpse over the edge of the suffocating quilt, because she knew the faces of the dead waited, their eyes pleading for attention, attention that she was afraid to give.

She knew! she silently shouted in disbelief.

She was so angry at the fact that her grandmother had known, and more than angry, she was resentful. Night after night she had suffered without sleep, fear controlling her mind and body.

She had refrained from making friends and having a boyfriend, and all because she was certain they would think she was crazy if they discovered her secret. But, to discover her grandmother suspected she was able to communicate with the dead. To realise, that she had experience of the paranormal via her mother, Mary's great grandmother, and that she could have given her advice and support in dealing with her fears.

This realisation shook Mary to her very core, and in doing so made her doubt the relationship they shared. She shook her head, pushing away her doubts, because if she lost faith in their relationship, she lost faith in everything she had ever known, and she just couldn't face that.

She returned to the question, *why now?* After all this time; why had she confided in Dawn? Something had changed. She couldn't quite fathom what; not yet at least, well, apart from the spirit which had appeared yesterday. It was like nothing she had ever witnessed before, and she knew, deep down, that this time she couldn't ignore the plea for help.

"Mary...*Are* you okay?" Dawn asked her, concern apparent in the quiver of her voice.
"Yes...yes, of course I *am*. Sorry. I was miles away." Mary smiled up at Dawn, and took a sip of her hot sweet tea, hoping it would reassure the older woman that she was okay. Instantly, Mary saw the frown fade from Dawn's worried brow, and a sweet smile of relief replacing it.
"Oh, my dear girl, I was a little worried for a while there...so will you tell me why you decided to admit to um...your...um…gift…at this particular time?"

"A spirit visited me last night, Dawn...He was so very scared. He was like a whirlwind, he confused me by how fast he spun, and I got the impression, although he didn't say it, that he had died violently." She paused, once more looking up at Dawn, who was holding her hand to her mouth in shock.

"I found it difficult to understand him...but I did get *one* word, a word he shouted over and over." Mary paused again, she then continued in a tiny whisper, "Kate, he called for *Kate!*"

Dawn sharply inhaled a startled gasp, "Do you think he meant Kate...you know, *our* Kate?"

"I don't know...But, I tried to call this morning and her mobile went to voicemail. I left a message, and I've left three more since, but she hasn't called back, and it's not like her.

I know it's ridiculous, because it might have nothing to do with Kate, but I think I need to go to London, I need to see her."

"Yes, yes, love I think you do. It's probably nothing, like you said. But even so, a trip to London will put your mind at ease, and I think it will do you good to take a holiday, have a little fun..."

Rising from the chair; Mary said, her voice nervous, "I'm going to go, I'm gonna get packed and set off before I can change my mind." Before Dawn was able to answer, she ran from the kitchen, up the stairs, and shouted back, "Call me a taxi, please."

Chapter Three

Mary quickly found a seat on the train and slumped down with a sigh. Her heart thumped hard in her chest from rushing around in preparation for the stay at Kate's. Well, she hoped she was going to be able to stay at Kate's, she still hadn't managed to get through to her, and her concerns were growing.

Feeling hot and bothered, Mary shrugged off her coat, and placed it on the rack overhead which also held her holdalls. She knew why she felt hot and bothered, it was the thought of entering London - she hated the place. The crowds of nameless people and spirits, pushing and shoving, it overwhelmed her, and made her feel claustrophobic and breathless. She found it embarrassing that she had, in the past, talked to spirits thinking they were alive and normal, only to realise that she was in fact talking to a dead person. More than once she had wanted to run away, when spectators to the event, as there were on several occasions, started to snicker and point at her, obviously thinking she was completely deluded.

However, this wasn't the only reason.

More than anything she was nervous at the thought of mixing with Kate's friends. For the most part Mary found them to be pompous, ignorant, and egotistical. She knew they only talked to her because they hoped she could further their career. However, when they realised she couldn't, they would promptly walk away, leaving her without concern or apology. She had on several occasions remarked to Kate on the shallowness of the company she kept. Kate would just laugh and say, "Oh, Mary, you need to get a thicker skin, it's not about you, it's just the way it is, it's called networking."

"I'm not stupid!" Mary would snap, "But is there a need to be quite *so* rude and ill mannered?" Kate would often shrug her shoulders and say, "It's the world I live and work in, Mar..."

Mary knew that after taking over her father's business of being an agent to the rich and famous, Kate, in fact, had no other choice but to associate with the rabble (Mary's name for Kate's associates and friends), and sometimes she felt guilty for her criticism of them. She knew that Kate was sometimes hurt by her remarks, she could tell by the expressions on her face, and she was certain that Kate thought that she was criticising her career.

Several times, Mary had tried to rectify this by adding that she knew Kate wasn't like them, but she just didn't like the crowd Kate hung out with. Mary, however, wasn't very good at expressing herself, especially under pressure, and so she normally ended up sounding even more scathing and dismissive of Kate's work than she did previously.

Trying unsuccessfully to snuggle down further into the unyielding chair, Mary looked around the carriage. It was empty. The one person other than her, who had been seated in the carriage when she had entered at Petersfield, got off a couple of stops later, which meant that Mary had the carriage to herself. She therefore hoped that no one else would enter, but knew that it was unlikely, so she closed her eyes and enjoyed the peace while she could.

Her eyes were only closed for about five minutes when she felt an overwhelming sense of rage enter. The hairs on the back of her arms and her neck stood on end, and her heart started to beat wildly in response to the presence. Mary spun around, trying to see the entity, but panicking because she couldn't see the spirit. The malice that engulfed her was almost palpable and her body shivered in fear in response to the entity.

Suddenly she was shoved with extreme force into the back of the chair, her arms held firmly in place by the invisible enemy.

"*Leave...go home...go home...go home, go home, go home, go home, gogogogoGOGOGOGOGOGOOOOOOOOOO OOOOOOOOOOO.*"

The high pitched scream echoed with needle-sharp pain in Mary's ears. She wanted to wrap her arms around her head; but was unable to, due to the spirit's weight bearing down on her body holding her in place. *Oh my God!* she silently screamed, unable to shout due to the pressure on her chest. *What is it, oh dear God, what is it?*

"*Leave, go...I will kill you...go home, go home, gogogogoGOGOGOGOGOGOGOOOOOOO OOOOOOOOOOOOOO.*"

Over and over the bellowing rant engulfed her senses, drowning her mind and body in its icy cold grip. Mary felt her mind descending into a black hole, spiralling down, down into an abyss that she struggled against, but couldn't climb out of, and the only escape was to give in and allow it to consume her.

<<<<>>>>

She's running along a sandy beach, the warm breeze tugging gently at her long dark hair, lifting it and caressing her long neck like a lover's kiss. She laughs in abandonment and it's a sound filled with joy and wonder. Suddenly the magical scene is shattered by the bellow of a gruff voice. The girl turns sharply. She's afraid of the man, and although she knows him well - he stalks her day and night. She turns reluctantly from the water's edge and starts to trudge back towards him. The key in her mind turns the lock inside her prison, the fun is gone, and once again she returns to a place that for her is hell - a place no child should inhabit.

<<<<>>>>

Mary gasps for breath as she rises up from the abyss into which she had fallen. Forgetting that she is, in fact, on a train, she jumps up off the seat and then suddenly falls back, unsteady on her feet from the lurching of the carriage.

"*What was that?*" she whispers to the empty space, but of course, no one answers. She quickly scans the now sterile and empty carriage, the air is still, and there is no sign of the menacing intruder.

Closing her eyes, she leans back against the scratchy textured fabric of the chair, a breath escaping her lips in a long, drawn-out sigh.

"We are approaching Woking station. Please stay in your seats until the train stops."

The unnatural sounding train voice startles Mary, and she feels her heart speed up, and places her hand to her chest to still the rapid beating. *What's happening to me?* she silently asks. Fear and trepidation concerning this new and unknown element of her 'gift', alarms her, and now more than ever she inwardly raves against the curse.

Raking her hands through her hair, she tries to steady her nerves.
"Bloody hell! Get a grip!" she mutters irritably to herself as she stands up and pulls the two large holdalls off the overhead rack in preparation for leaving the train. The next stop being Clapham Junction, the change she needs to make in order to get to Victoria Station, which was just a few minutes' walk from Kate's apartment.

Well, let's hope I make it to Kate's without the added bonus of thousands of ghosts, her inner voice shouts, *and in one piece would be even better,* she adds scathingly.

About the author

Having run a successful garden centre then a floristry business, Charmain Mitchell never really had time to concentrate on her passion for writing.

Throughout her life, Charmain had wanted to become an author, but family and business commitments stood in the way and her writing consisted of a few short stories on the rare occasion that she had time to write them.

In late 2012, a freak accident finally allowed time for Charmain to indulge in her passion for writing. She says of this; "Then a few weeks ago I fell over whilst trying to catch chickens and ended up breaking my ankle! Quite a comical way to break your ankle - I know; especially when I have kept horses for the majority of my life and have never yet broken any bones where they are concerned!

Suddenly I had six clear weeks in which I wouldn't be able to move very well. Help! How was I going to cope with doing zilch for that long? Then I thought, maybe I should do a bit of writing, and that is what I did, and the strange thing is, is that I haven't been able to stop since!"

She says of her writing;

"I love writing, it is truly my passion! I love the way that through words I can make people think and feel differently, feel passion, sometimes pain, and get totally lost in my words. I love the fact that a brilliant writer will live forever, and will in some way influence generations to come. Is it not marvelous that we can still look back to writing from over two thousand years ago and believe in it and still learn from it?

The human imagination is a wondrous thing, it creates and then brings to life stories on a screen, and sometimes we believe in these stories so much that they become our passion. I'm talking about for instance: the lord of the rings, harry potter, and star wars etc... I think we actually forget sometimes that all of these stories were started with a simple idea on a piece of paper, and they grew to be something that some of us forget started from the author's imagination."

Charmain Mitchell lives in a semi-rural village on the south coast of the UK with her four children, husband, two cats, and countless chickens, duck, geese and turkeys.

If you would like to follow Charmain, you can do so via the following:

Twitter:
https://twitter.com/charmain_m

Facebook:

https://www.facebook.com/GwenVampire

Blog:
http://charmainmitchell.blog.co.uk/

Or you can drop Charmain a line at:
cmmpublishing@gmail.com

Made in the USA
Middletown, DE
27 November 2017